# ORADOUR

## A Village at War

## Brian Francis

*To the villagers of Oradour and the people of Dresden.*
*All victims of war.*

# CONTENTS

# ACKNOWLEDGMENTS

A tale of Two Cities.  Charles Dickens.

World at War ITV Series.

The Village of Oradour/Centre des Martyrs.

Mary Higginson: encouraging me to write this work.

Anya Goulden:  assisting with illustration.

My son Adam for having to listen to his father's ripping yarns.

*Freedom is when one hears the bell at seven o'clock in the morning and knows it is the milkman and not the Gestapo.*

GEORGES BIDAULT

# PROLOGUE

Winter tests everything. It reshapes the land, tearing it apart particle by particle. It creates its own mood, as if to say, 'Here I am again and maybe this time I will stay forever.' Solitude becomes a watchword. There is no escape and nowhere to go, either. Winter is a serious business. For some it is the silence. For others it is about death and a time for waiting until the spring. Surviving the winter is the ultimate test of everything and everyone.

As temperature falls molecules cease to vibrate, motion slows and particles move into a defensive mode. The cold loosens their connections and memory dies. There is no retrieving such knowledge when the cold goes away. It is not recovered by the warmth of the sun. Sometimes the particles fall away completely and they have no further part to play. They understand that they must now take their chances with all of the others as the returning warm breeze relocates them across surfaces and funnels them into drains and streams. They are disconnected from the whole. They leave in their millions every day. But they will have to wait for the warmth to return before they begin their journey again. Right now they are locked in place.

Animals can find no water. It is protected from their scent and inability to use a tool. There is no nourishment for them either. The birds leave and wait out the storm. Fish breathe with shallowness and wait for a little sun to open the water way so they can gasp for a few more moments at life. They will die tonight if the sun loses the fight.

The wind rips away the surface, but it, too, has another part to play. It makes the earth tidy. The debris of nature is blown to one place and there it stays. Surfaces of fields are taken to the edge and the sticks of the crops are taken away and stored in corners or hedges for others to make use of them.

They become a bank of useful materials for smaller creatures that live on the edges of existence and have to fight hard to survive. The wind strips the trees of last year's leaves and dead branches fall. Any leftover fruit falls to take its chances with the hard earth. The wind creates the space for early light to penetrate the branches and force buds into activity. In the winter the trees are no longer aware of themselves. They sleep. Some cannot fight the penetration of the cold and if it reaches their core they die. They are still useful as they will become the warmth of the future in some hearth or grate. Then they, too, will begin their journey to return from whence they came. Already things are ahead of them. Already small creatures living amongst the fallen leaves begin to awaken at the change of events. They are not yet ready, but they are fooled into believing that they have reached the leaf mould early and are now making it their serious business to find a mate and start their cycle again, dying in their millions before they find each other. Only a few are needed to evidence the fact that the species is still present. It has not gone away to oblivion. The trees know their role. They have been on the earth for thousands of millions of years. They are there long before creatures emerged from the sea to live in the mud and swamps. They ruled the earth with majesty, setting a perfect example for those who came later to choose to ignore. They understand the waiting and being abused and yet being useful. They are the true and only collectors of the sun's energy, as they return year after year to enrich the soil, provide homes for the flying creatures and protect the land, locking into place the very particles that are sometimes blown away by the blistering wind and flood waters. The trees have only one real fear: fire.

# PART ONE

I Am The Village.

My walls have stood for hundreds, for thousands, of summers and winters. I have kept my people cool, or warm, as they have journeyed through the seasons of their lives. They have protected generations of simple folk who worked the land, and received from it the bounty for which all small communities hope and pray. From a distance everything here would appear the same. I remember the soldiers coming home from the Great War, and those that did not. Their names are listed on one of my ruined walls. They would still know me, even now. Those that did not die came home damaged; they were years in my keeping before they were the same again. Some never are; their scars are both physical and mental. It is difficult for me to judge which is worse - I am only a village. I remember Georges standing in the distance. He is instantly recognisable. He has the biggest hands that have ever touched me. They have carefully placed mortar between the stones that helped to create me. They are clean, gentle hands, but tough and strong, the kind of hands that a young woman seeking a husband would find attractive. They have the skills to build a home for children. They can do a day's work and more. He has a good eye too, they say. He can build a perpendicular wall without a plumb line, using the horizon and the church tower as his guide as he works. His brother put the roofs on. I never heard his brother's sing-song voice again after the survivors came home from the war. I remember hearing their mother crying softly every night in her empty bed. I remember her shrieks when she sees Georges on the top of the hill that overlooks this village. She is looking through the window and I feel drops of salt water fall on my honey-coloured stone window sill. Georges is standing, surveying the village that is part of him and he, too, is a part of it. His uniform now carries three stripes and the colours of a Croix de Guerre. Georges cannot believe that he has made it home.

The answer to his question about Mr Denis's fine wine shop is, "Yes, it is still there," and, "Yes, it could be opened for a soldier coming home from war." This seems fair to us both, for he has formed the sign in the stone at the door of the shop. Chez Denis had been a local joke at the time, but I fail to understand its significance. Everyone knows about the fine wines and spirits. A little dilution here and there, but who is to tell? Everyone knows where the missing fraction goes, but M. Denis has much to carry, and the spirit to bear it, usually yours.

Georges' chisel feels cool as it removes layers of stone from my surfaces that have been millions of years in the making. Every strike of the well-worn hammer on the stonemason's chisel shakes apart bonds that formed eons ago in the folding earth. His breath on my stone blows gently, removing small particles of sand and dust to start their journey again. And in those hands, cool in the evening of a warm summer's day, I feel something else too: pride.

If he had turned at that moment he would have seen a petite, dark-haired admirer gazing at him in the evening sunshine. She has watched him since she was a little girl. She is now a woman, a young woman, but a woman nevertheless. He has probably never noticed her, she is thinking, but in fact it is clear that the opposite has already happened. He had gone to war as a shy young man and come back feeling much older. He observes her one day hanging out the family washing.

Many marriages occur within villages at this time. Many are pre-arranged, although the intended couple never know until years later. But this is after the Great War when men have died in their millions on the Western Front. I have exactly one hundred names on my church wall. You can still visit me and see the names of all of my children. You can see them all over France. Many of the names are matching in pairs and triplicates. They are brothers in life and now in death. He looked many times at his brother's name. It could have been him. It should have been him. His brother was the chosen one, the one who would make good and become something other than a stonemason, a builder, or a carpenter. The war stopped all that. They could not even find his body after the battle. Their mother never gives up hope.

I have never been physically touched by war. I have never really known devastation of any kind, not since the first of my people settled here. They came from the East and spoke a beautiful, poetic language that sounded like the movement of the water in the falls that are nearby. They made camp and built the first defences from stones that are simply part of the earth. They joined the stones together and so I came into being.

Other wars came and went, as did these men, but they left their poetry behind, not just with the ones who remained but in the stone itself. At first there are only deep voices that made my stones vibrate powerfully. They called each other soldiers and each group of ten had a leader. They laughed a lot and made jokes about each other and when they wanted to insult their friends they made up stories about what their wives were doing while they were away. It was probably the same as what they did with the local girls. Sometimes the insults would come after they drank something that was not water and then they fought with each other, often ending up in the river and the mud of the nearby fields. It was on days like this that the local girls usually had to watch out. The next day they were often ill and their leaders did a lot of shouting. They still worked. They put down floors, built walls and then added roofs.

Fields were marked out and others came to work in them. They planted crops and vines, built a wall across the river, and when the water level rose enough they used it for their needs. They made their own waterfall. The water cascaded slowly in shiny lances of silver, like fish flicking through the water. They spent a lot of time there, often sleeping during the hottest of days. They dream of their homes and families in a place that is far away in distance and memory. They cleaned their clothes and washed themselves in the larger pool that they had caused to form.

They came and went, never the same people. Perhaps they went home. Who knows? Then one day they all left just as the sun started to rise. They never returned. They left behind their villas and barns, and the fruits of their liaisons with the local girls. In the soil they left their dead, buried with their swords and valuables. These relics are still here, as they have been for thousands of years now. I know exactly where they are. If it were possible I would tell you their names and of their wives and children and their dreams.

At first the workers in the fields never noticed that their masters had gone, but once they had understood that they were alone and free from bondage, they stayed and occupied the village. They had learned the language of the soldiers and now spoke a new lyrical language of their own. The soldiers would still understand it even if they returned today. They were clever too. They had skills that they had never been asked to use; many of them had trades and could build houses, forge metal and make weapons and useful tools. They joined the fields together with paths that were made for trade but not for a marching army. They brought their produce to trade in a small field by the river just at the edge of the village which they had already occupied. They traded with each other and began to add their own buildings where they could sell things. Leather, polished stones, metal tools for working the fields. Some were so successful that they gave up their fields for an amount of the produce. Farming became a little easier and so did their lives. Food was plentiful. They traded horses, cattle and goats. Their wives began to make fine cloth. Nothing that was produced was ever wasted. For hundreds of years they remained undisturbed apart from outsiders who traded and left. They heard of disturbing things in far off places but this village was hidden, and was not yet ready to change a single thing.

***

Georges had a final unanswered question: what would his mother think when she saw his uniform, which was by now beyond even her repair skills? His right arm is folded upwards to his shoulder; an index finger acts as a hook to support his heavy soldier's tunic, now with the markings of a sergeant's stripes and the colours of the Croix de Guerre stitched to his left breast. The tunic is weighted further by the medal in a soldier's tin, with the bits and bobs of war collected by all men out in the field; an unfired German bullet that failed to go off and kill him at point-blank range; the German soldier's cap badge, left behind as he fled without his rifle and cap and dignity, but with the reminder of how close he came to death, too. The scar of a bayonet in his rear end will be his sole reminder of this day. Georges admired his bravery as he appeared to lead the charge right up to their lines on what was to become the last day of the war. Men dropped all around him but he made it to the forward French trenches, his rifle jamming as he pointed it at Georges. He turned slowly to either side and realised that he was alone, but some thought of survival passed through his mind and it showed in his chlorine-damaged eyes. He threw his rifle at Georges, who caught it neatly with both hands, bayonet pointing at the small man with a dark moustache to match. They both became aware that the firing had stopped. A brutal split second passed between them. For the soldiers in the French trenches an order to cease fire gave the small German corporal a chance to retreat, but not before he had been given an ignominious final prod, with his own bayonet, in his own rear end, to be on his way.

"That's for trying to spoil things." Georges was aware that the fighting was close to an end. Rumour had it that the Germans were suing for an armistice. Georges looked at the small distance between the opposing trenches, once again strewn with the dead and dying. He looked carefully at the well-made German rifle and opened the breech to reveal the intact cartridge with a strike mark on it. He removed it gently and placed it on the firing shelf next to his tobacco tin. He stored the rifle and wondered if this would be perhaps one of the final actions of the war. Sure enough, three hours later the order to withdraw to the main trench was given. An officer was waiting for them.

"You are all going home boys. It's over."

It was as simple as that. He looked around the trench that had been his home, off and on, for nearly a year. He went to a workbench and carefully withdrew the bullet from the brass casing. He had intended to pour out the black gunpowder that had not ignited, but some ancient machine in some far away factory had failed to deliver its charge and the small German corporal had been fighting with nothing more than a lance, which, when Georges returned to the brightness of the main trench, had disappeared into someone else's collection. That was soldiers for you. One minute they were defending your life as if you matter more than they do and next they steal your wife as if they were there first. Now they were all going home, and someone was leaving with his rifle. He looked at his carefully constructed trench. He had a well-earned reputation as a number one trench builder, even amongst the enemy. He applied his knowledge of building to the trenches, careful cross members keeping the soft walls in place. Roofing techniques applied to the bracing of walls. His brother had taught him well.

He looked at the many roofs his brother had put on the houses he had built and the additions they had added when babies had arrived, the familiar bell-tower of the church that his grandfather had built. He could see his own home and thought he saw his mother at his old bedroom window when a silver-grey haired rocket in black hurtled from the front door and started to sprint up the street.

He remained at the top of the rise and waited for his mother to arrive; the colours of the early morning dew were disappearing from the long grass as she reached him. It was incredible. He had never seen his mother run before. She stopped an arm's length away, checking that her eyes had not betrayed her. He saw her making familiar gestures with her hands that he remembered from when he was a small boy. She was turning her wrists, holding her hands out open and flat with the thumb placed into its palm. Then, both hands open, waited for him. He walked into her embrace and into the body that had given him life.

"You are home now."

"Yes mama. I am."

***

His breakfast is on the familiar kitchen table. The smells of home are still the same. Polished waxed furniture mixes with a slight fragrance of railway stations that he has never been able to explain. But this is no departure. This is home. His mother wastes no time.

"You know Celine's fiancé was killed at Mézièrs. She was supposed to marry him this weekend. All the other younger girls in the village are spoken for if their men come home."

She continues to prepare the food as Georges listens as his mother lists the young ladies of the village and soon realises that there are none that he wishes to marry. They had been his friends at school and are more like sisters to him. She cannot contain her joy that her son is a hero and that he has survived. She knows that she should be grateful that one of her sons has made it home, as some of the other families have lost all of their sons.

*\*\**

Hannah knows the first time Heinz kisses her.

She has been kissed before, but not like this. She returns his gentle kiss willingly. He holds her close and places his hands to her cold cheeks. She feels warm and wanted, desired.

"I must go," she says, and moves towards the steps that lead to her parents' house.

He looks into her clear grey eyes, brushes the small curls from her face, tracing the line of her smile. "Not yet."

"I have had a lovely evening, but I must go. My father will expect me home soon."

"A lovely evening? Coffee and cake in the park? A walk by the river. Not very much for a first evening."

"A first kiss."

"Yes."

"I enjoyed our conversation. You are very unusual. You still know how to think for yourself."

"I would like to see you again."

She stands on the lower step and whispers into his ear, "Only again?"

She kisses him and slips away up the worn stone steps of her parents' home, closing the door firmly behind her. The click of the latch echoes through the silent house, placing a formal barrier between her racing pulse and the young man outside, who still sees her image through the heavy wooden door. He waits until the lights are switched on and off, and on and off, and the house is in final darkness. Her father will now know she is home. She has raced to her bedroom so that she can catch a final glimpse of her handsome young man and so make her evening last a little longer. If he had waited for a few more moments he would have noted that in the darkness, through the smallest slit in the closed curtains, she had watched him walk slowly away from her as a light spring rain begins to run down the glass window, interrupting her view and thoughts.

As the damp night closes around him, he too is thinking, and he cannot hide the joy he is feeling. His hand caresses the book in his otherwise nearly empty pocket. He can feel the smoothness of the well-worn leather cover, its corners no longer sharp, spine flaking, leaving behind minute pieces of evidence in the debris found in any pocket of any well-worn coat. He can feel the indentations of the gold-pressed letters of her name on its cover and is pleased to know that its surface will still contain the imprint of her hand, reminding him of how they held hands briefly under the table - almost accidentally at first and later awkwardly, gradually finding a comfort in each other's presence. He removed his leather gloves and touched her face before kissing her. She returned his kiss, of that he is sure.

"Please look after my book." The other, often unspoken half of any human bargain, aside from love: trust. She slid the book of poems into his pocket, an invitation to meet again.

His joy is short-lived as he reaches his home to find a telegram recalling him from leave.

***

On her way home from work Hannah places the flowers Heinz had given to her on to her mother's grave. She often visits this place of tranquillity to seek advice from her mother. She knows already what her mother would think.

"Mama, I'm in love."

"You're so young."

"I am eighteen. You were eighteen when you met papa."

"That was different. Good, healthy men were in short supply. You've just got your first job - a good job too. Jobs are hard to come by in Dresden."

"That is where I met him. He was looking for a first edition book for his mother's birthday. I found it for him. He said he was going to a concert in the park this evening. He asked me go with him." Her mother would have frowned but also noticed how alive and happy her daughter's expressive face suddenly appeared.

"Your father took me to the best restaurant for our first time together, and he asked my father first."

Hannah sighs to herself. She knows the story well and that her father had taken her mother for coffee without asking granddad for permission of any sort.

"Mama, we walked along the river and then listened to part of the concert. He does not talk like other boys. He reads books. He listens to music. He wants to become an architect."

"So you will see him again?"

"Tomorrow, I hope." And tomorrow, and the day after that, she thinks.

She had given him her personal copy of her favourite book of poems. She knows he will return it. It is signed and dated by her grandfather. 'To Hannah, My little dreamer, love Opa, Christmas 1936.' Three years ago already. It is a personal item, part of her. If he rejects it so be it. She is testing him. She knows he will be waiting for her at lunchtime on the park bench.

He knows it is a test too. Her book is on her desk the next morning with a note inside; in part an explanation of why he cannot meet her for a while.

***

"The story is in the eye of the beholder, not the writer."

She has paused in her own train of thought to consider this view of literature, described to her in this way for the first time. It is an impressive statement made by an equally impressive man. Good looking, too; she cannot help but notice other females, married or not, young or old, making exactly the same judgement. She notices the envious looks that they aim at her as they flick their eyes over the rest of the person with whom she is linking her arm. He is equally impressive with his clean, well-cared for hands. She likes the neat hands that gesture so well to explain his words. She has already imagined those hands on her body, but knows he is a gentleman. Still, she wonders what he will think if she makes it obvious that she wants him. The thought of them together like that makes her feel warm. She looks at the hands again as he removes the debris from a park bench lunch that the birds have not yet found. She sits in the space he has created for her. He sits to her left and takes hold of her gloved right hand, causing her to turn gently and face him. He lets her hand drop to her lap and moves his hand to her face.

"I would like to kiss you now."

She places her free hand to his shirt; his heart is pounding. She looks at him and closes her eyes. He kisses her gently. She is pleased. It is exactly the sort of kiss that is just about acceptable in public. It is a pleasant kiss and she returns it with exactly the same feeling. Her only other act of intimacy is to allow his forehead to meet hers.

"I think you are wonderful."

There, he has said it and she has thought it. She squeezes his hand and allows her head to slip into the crook of his shoulder. His left hand holds her right hand. He holds her very close and she is an exact fit for the shape of his neck and shoulder. She hopes he will know that this means she feels the same way.

"The writer proposes the words, and puts them in the order that they desire, to convey their meaning. Then we put our own understanding on the words within our own context and interpretation."

"What would your reader think if she had read the words in your story that said, 'Kiss me again'?" She places a finger to his lips to silence him. He gives the most correct and simplest of interpretations. He does not speak. She is pleased with loveliness of his kiss. There is a time for talking and a time for kissing, and for this moment the time for talking is over. She returns his kiss and melts into him.

She folds his letter and places it carefully back in its envelope again.

He has told her that he understands one thing above all else: he wants to be with her. So he had started his letter with those very words. She tries hard to remember the times they have spent together so far.

\*\*\*

She is unaware that a large man sitting opposite is staring at her, as she is absorbed by the interest of a newly chosen book. Her grandfather's book of poems is next to her, but as yet unread. There is a note tucked into a particular page - a book mark. The note reads, 'My favourite; reminds me of you.' It is signed, *Heinz*. She is astonished at this choice. Her grandfather had said the same thing as he had read it to her. Did Heinz make a good guess? If not, the coincidence is amazing.

The large man sits down next to her, at a proper distance.

"What are you reading, may I ask?"

The question is friendly enough and not uncommon in a park often full of people eating their lunches and reading a book or newspaper. The man is not quite old enough to be her father, but not young enough to be of interest to a young woman - especially this one. She thinks she has met the right man for her already.

"May I see?"

The gap closes. She feels uncomfortable. This had not been the case when she and Heinz first kissed. She had wanted to be even closer to him. She had wanted to melt into him and their legs had touched too when he had kissed her for the first time. This older man now allows his leg to casually fall against hers. She moves away, rapidly. She is now at the very end of the bench. She has chosen to sit here so that she can remember the previous evening. Heinz's note contains a simple explanation as to why he had not been able to meet her. She places her hand to her lips and wishes he was here right now. She can still feel the moment their lips separated. He had then kissed her eyes, the tip of her nose and another gentle lingering touch of their lips. How can this happen so quickly? She is in love already and knows it.

The unwanted guest on their bench is now reading Heinz's note.

She snatches it from his grasp. "How dare you!"

"This man, he should not be telling you where he is serving. You could both get into trouble."

"I do not know where he is serving. He was recalled by his regiment. And I do not know who he serves with either."

"You do not know much about this man, do you?"

"I know what I need to know."

"A young woman like you needs someone nearby, who can take care of her and see to her needs, not someone who might be killed at any moment."

His friendly tone has now disappeared and she is very uncomfortable in this man's presence. She can smell alcohol on his breath.

She stands up and tries to remove the book from his hand. She notices the swastika pin in his lapel.

"Just who are you?" She shouts loudly, hoping other passersby will hear.

"How rude of me." He was about to kiss her hand and introduce himself, but she pulls her hand away. "I am someone who needs to know about soldiers who tell their girls about where they are serving. I suppose you would call me an observer; a watcher of people and their habits."

"My book," she insists.

"Your name, his name," he demands, covering his actions, fingering his party badge in his lapel.

"You know his name." She turns to walk away.

"Yes, his and another man's name are in your book; and he is your grandfather."

She looks him the eye. "Then you have all I know and need to know. My book, please," she says loudly enough to now attract the attention of the passersby.

He gives her the book and taps his forehead in a knowing way. "We shall meet again."

As she walks back to the shop she realises she is shaking like a leaf. Heinz had written his note on the back of a bill from the book shop.

Heinz finds the fat Gestapo Agent quickly. Hannah's description in her terror had been clear enough. He needs his rage to carry out his intentions. The bar on Fredrick Strasse is busy. He sees him sitting in the corner; he is smoking and drinking, smiling with his friends, nodding and making lewd gestures. He moves to the same corner and can hear the Gestapo agent bragging about what he has just done to a girl - a Jewish girl. Heinz now realises why she has not confided in him before.

He had found her at the back of the book shop. Her blouse was torn, her face marked. She looked child-like. She could not control her limbs. He was enraged.

"Who did this?" he demanded.

"I don't know his name," she sobbed into his shoulder.

He kissed her on the forehead and tried to quieten her. "Did he…?"

"No."

He looked at her beautiful, marked faced. He kissed the bruising and brushed away the hair clouding her face. He pulled her torn blouse together to cover her naked breasts. He put his coat around her shoulders. He was still in full uniform. He had not been able to wait to get home. His mates had laughed at him.

"She must be worth it," they had joked.

"You have no idea."

He locked the door to the shop.

"Do you have any brandy?"

"Schnapps." He poured them both a drink.

"It is him again. He keeps coming back. I don't know what to do."

"I do. I will be back shortly."

He had known exactly where the fat slob would be. He checks that his sidearm is not loaded.

"So, you like defenceless girls?"

No one moves.

"You," he says. "Stand up." He draws his sidearm and points it at him. He is standing now. "So, you like to rape defenceless girls?"

"I didn't rape her," the white-faced man says. "Anyway, she was begging for it." He smirks, looking around the room for support, taking courage from the many grinning faces, unaware they are more amused more by his situation than what his story contains.

"What, with you? Do your friends know you like little boys too? Do you tell them when you bugger little boys?"

White changes to purple in the blink of an eye. Heinz waves the unloaded gun across the crowded room. Everyone cowers, heads lower than table tops. They have noted the Iron Cross and the black Waffen SS uniform - and the rage of a serving soldier.

"Let me explain something to you - all of you." Heinz pauses for breath, amazed at his power. *This is how she has made you feel*, a little voice warns.

"I do not want to have to shoot you, any of you, but if you or anyone else goes near her again I will arrange for you to be sent to the East." The bar begins to empty. Fatso is on his knees and now isolated. He leans forward and whispers in his ear, "Believe me I will kill you if I have to." He releases him and allows him to stand.

"Jew lover."

In one motion Heinz turns and fires. A loud click resonates through the still silent bar. The empty gun says nothing and everything. He watches the fat man's face change as a large, wet stain spreads from his groin.

"Call yourself a man. Look at you. You're pathetic," he says, smiling and pointing the gun, drawing circles with its barrel at the man's groin. He puts the gun away. Fear is a great thing.

"Don't worry about your daughters, but make sure you warn your sons about this man's taste for little boys."


"Why didn't you tell me?"

"I was afraid I would lose you."

"You may lose me anyway."

"But that would be our choice. My great grandma is Jewish. None of my grandparents are Jewish. I am classed as a full German, so is my brother. I never thought about it. I knew I had distant Jewish ancestry, but I did not think it would matter. I am not even a Mischling."[1]

"It might, but not to me." The complexity of his own words does not even register with him; love is blind, after all.

She rests her head on his. She sleeps and so does he. They sleep like lovers. He has come home to kiss her and hold her and talk with her, but this is more than enough. He has never been this close to another human being. The way she has pulled his arm across her like a bed cover for comfort, her body formed within his embrace, tells him she feels the same way.

"And who might you be, young man?" They both awake, startled, realising how this looks.

"Father."

"Sir, this is not how it appears."

"And how would you like it to appear?" Her father has taken note of the torn blouse, which she is quickly adjusting.

"Daddy, this is the gentleman I have been telling you about."

"Gentleman? What has happened to you? Has he done this to you? Your face, it is marked. Young man, get out, now. Some gentleman. Look at the state of my daughter. Look at what have you done to her. How dare you? Get out of my house right now and do not come back."

Heinz stands up. "Sir, I have nothing but honourable intentions towards your daughter. I am not responsible for what has happened. If I am guilty of anything it is the fact that I arrived too late to stop it."

"Father, he defended me."

"Looks like he did not do a very good job." Her father says, starting to calm down. "What are your intentions towards my little girl?"

"Sir, I love her. I wish to marry her, if you will give your permission." He squeezes Hannah's hand.

---

[1] A Mischling is someone with Jewish ancestry with one (2nd degree) or two (1st degree) grandparents who are considered Jewish. Hannah would have been considered as being not Jewish at all and would have in reality probably applied to be seen as Aryan. However there are fanatics of racial purity who did not accept this basic ideology and are willing to cause problems for others. There are also people who abused their powers for their own gain.

"What does my little girl think of that?"

"I feel the same way." She squeezes his hand back. It is the strangest proposal of marriage ever, she thinks. She feels safe. He makes her feel safe, just like her father.

"Are you asking me for my daughter's hand in marriage?"

"Yes, sir."

"You know that if you ever harm my daughter or allow her to be harmed in any way, you will answer to me."

Heinz feels like every young man in history who has done this most difficult thing. "Yes, sir."

Hannah smiles. She looks at her future husband and kisses his hand.

"Have you bought her a ring?"

"Not yet, sir."

"Wait here, and stop calling me sir. I was never an officer. I had more sense. Top soldier though."

Heinz looks at his future wife. "What do I call him?"

"You'll think of something - as long as it is not father."

He holds her close. "I am sorry."

She places a finger to his lips and kisses him. "No need. Anyone who can face my father in these circumstances is always going to be my hero."

"It is supposed to be romantic, an unforgettable occasion."

"What can be more unforgettable than this, and to be asked in front of my father?"

"I was going to ask you if you would have my babies."

"I think you already have." She kisses him again as her father returns to the room.

"Leave each other alone for a moment. I guess neither of you will have any money saved. Young people these days, too impetuous by half. It would please me immensely young man if... I don't even know your name."

"Heinz."

"It would please me immensely, Heinz, if you would allow my daughter to wear this ring, which I bought for her mother when we were betrothed. It would only be temporary, of course, until you can afford to buy your own."

"I would be honoured." And before he can ask Hannah if it is acceptable she holds her hand out. She knows it will be a perfect fit. She has tried it on many times, especially since her mother died. She knows where her mother's wedding dress is too. It will need taking in here and there. Heinz takes a deep breath to stop the shaking and places the ring on her finger and he holds her hand out to her father.

"Sir, I love your daughter."

"So do I."

"And I love you both." She always did try to have the last word.

"Now sir, if you wish to court my daughter you may call me Joseph. So how come, young man, did you allow my daughter get into such a state?"

Joseph knows that this is not the last they will hear of the Gestapo Agent who is pursuing his daughter - and his future son-in-law's future wife. Eventually, one of them will have to deal with him.

"I think you should marry sooner rather than later. I think I would like grandchildren. Grandpa Joseph has a certain ring to it, don't you think so?"

For once he has the final word. Hannah goes to the attic just before he does. She is holding her mother's wedding dress against her own body. They smile at each other, sharing the special bond they have between them. Heinz is left in the kitchen with the remains of a bottle of schnapps. He needs a drink to calm his nerves. He, too, realises that the problem with the fat man is not yet over.

*** 

The countryside of Northern France is passing Julia by and she is most certainly not enjoying the experience. Most girls of her age do not want to visit relatives in the north but would rather be swimming in the lake with their friends, talking about boys who are ignoring them. Instead she is on a train close to the Belgium border. She is nearly fourteen and has no time for this. She flicks away the sharp curls that cover her eyes and sees the flat fields of the north.

"Cows, cows, cows. Boring, boring, boring." Her mother reads her thoughts.

At Lille it is different. *Les soldats d'Angleterre* are everywhere as the train pulls into the station, and they are handsome, handsome, handsome. Well, they are different, anyway. She quickly brushes her hair in the rail carriage window, hoping her curls do not make her look like a baby. She is aware that she looks older than her age. Some of her friends are still pulling faces at boys but she has crossed the divide. Her mother has noted the physical changes, too, and the attitude that comes with it. She knows her daughter well enough and notes her intense gaze.

"Julia, they are a little old for you my dear."

"If you say so, mama."

"I do." And she is immediately aware that these men in uniform are actually still boys. They can be no older than nineteen or twenty. She is old enough to be their mother. Many of these soldiers would have taken her for their mother as they are young and some are away from home for the first time in their lives. They are missing their homes - which, of course, means their mothers - but they are too proud to admit it to each other, covering their feelings with soldiers' banter. They cheerfully move out of the ladies' way as they alight from the train. Many of them of touch their caps as the ladies go by on the platform. Rumour has it that the young British soldiers are on their way to the Belgian border.

"Eyes front, young lady." But she, too, cannot resist a quick look. The officers are a little older.

"Caught you, mama." They both laugh, linking arms together with difficulty as her mother is carrying her little brother and a suitcase. Julia carries another case and they head towards the steam from the cooling engine at the buffered end of the platform. This is the end of the line. Georges is waiting for them beyond the ticket barrier. He takes his son from his wife's arms.

"We need to leave here urgently."

"We have only just arrived."

***

Frank is holding the lifeless body of his sister in his arms. Her cries woke him in the night and he sat with her until the dawn forced him to sleep. His cries now wake the household and he hears his mother's short intake of breath and quiet sob. His gaunt father, so strict and severe, is holding the child's hand, his eyes brimming as he kisses his only daughter on the forehead. Frank places his sister back on the bed. He brushes the curls away from her face; he touches her on the nose before kissing it. There will be no response to his usual form of teasing. No shouts of "Mum, tell him to stop." As he gently places her head on the pillow he recognises another voice.

*"I am speaking to you from the Cabinet Room at Ten Downing Street.*

*This morning the British Ambassador in Berlin handed the German Government a final note stating that, unless we hear from them by eleven o'clock that they are prepared at once to withdraw their troops from Poland, a state of war will exist between us. I have to tell you now that no such undertaking has been received, and that consequently this country is at war with Germany."*

Frank looks at the small bedside clock he bought for her last birthday. It is just after 11 a.m. His sister is dead - what did the Government think about that? The Poles are fighting for their lives and are holding their own against the Germans but now the Russians have invaded too. People are dying all over Poland but some still died during wars in perfectly ordinary ways; his sister is one of them.

\*\*\*

He hears a male voice shouting to take cover as the stretcher in his hands is pulled towards the side of the road. Large numbers of people, soldiers and civilians, are abandoning everything to search for some sort of protection. They are not able to run into the fields because of the wounded man on their stretcher. He can hear the sound of a plane begin its attack as the note of the engine whines to a sickening pitch; bullets pitch the ground, travelling faster than the single bomb about to explode. He sees a French family trying to protect each other. The man and woman are sheltering their children as best they can. A young girl looks at him from beneath the cover of a heavy black coat. She smiles at him and waves to him as she disappears in a cloud of dust, debris and death.

How far can a man walk in a day? Frank has just found out and it is not a calculation of distance but a measure of pain and exhaustion. But his muscles are warm and his body tingles. He feels very much alive. He has a sense of purpose unlike many of the others walking with them. His burden is heavy but it is at least shared. They have given up carrying their man-made stretcher in the normal manner. Blistered hands, raw and peeling skin bandaged on only with the extra socks their mothers had made for them, are no substitute, but at least their hands are now free. Aching tendons have been pulled to the limits of endurance. No food for two days now; water left for one. They are following the road but not quite on it. The roads are blocked with the last of the many retreating multitudes. They have not seen a working vehicle in the last day. The three servicemen are the only ones in the convoy in uniform. There would be no help to come. They are not armed and are not meant to be. Even soldiers with red crosses on their armbands are still a target. The wounded count for nothing. So they walk separately as best they can, away from the civilians, not wishing to cause them further problems.

They share the last of their water with the man on the stretcher and lie down in a field adjacent to a small convent. Frank would have willingly exchanged places with the still-unconscious pilot. They cover him as best they can and lie down in the furrows of the ploughed field. In the morning they will pick him up again and place the webbing from their uniforms around their necks that support the stretcher and carry on with the final leg of their journey.

They sleep in the early evening in the open near the convent. They say goodbye to their families and loves. He sees his sister again waving happily to him, her homemade dress fluttering in the slipstream created by the rope swing he made for her in the garden. Then she is covered with a large black coat and another face appears. She smiles confidently at him and this time he manages to wave back before she is shrouded in smoke and debris. He awakens, startled by the scene from his dream. It is still light. He checks the injured man and makes his way to the road, which is now completely deserted. He knows he has to get home but Dunkirk is still some distance away. His legs refuse to cooperate as he breaks into a jog. Anyone seeing his friend and the pilot will assume they are dead. Nearby, their fathers and uncles lie in another field. Their names on the crosses and stones are the final relics from another war of not so long ago. She has to still be there, he tells himself. If he can get back quickly he may still have a chance.

Frank went back. Despite carrying the wounded officer for the last twenty hours they managed to stop within the hour at the nearby convent in a small village. He tried to tell the family to wait for him to return. He is not a doctor but knows the signs of compression injuries - very nasty but not necessarily fatal. He finds the young girl at the side of the road covered in twigs and reeds and a man's coat. Her hair has been brushed and her face is clean. Her hands are joined and placed across her chest. A medal and Rosary beads placed around her neck complete the image of a child prepared for the final journey. He is a Catholic but also knows enough to know that this young girl is not yet ready to go anywhere - in itself a small miracle, but even more miraculous is the fact that the Germans, for some reason, appear to have stopped advancing.

Amidst the chaos and debris of the scattered belongings and burnt-out cars and carts he gathers her into his arms, and then on to his back to begin the hour-long journey back to the convent. The girl does not speak on their journey, although the movement has now awakened her. He cannot provide any information about her when he asks the nuns for help. No, he does not know her name; he knows nothing about her. The good sisters provided all the aid that they dared, but when he arrives with a young girl and he takes her to them, they need to go beyond daring. He asks them to look after her. They ask him to write down everything he can remember. He also puts a note in her pocket, thanking her for helping him to have courage when the bombs are falling, and telling her that she reminds him of his sister named Lucy, who also had great courage. The paper is weighed down with and folded over and around the medal. He signs it with his name, Francis. He is pleased with what he has done and hopes his dead sister will not mind him sharing something personal about her and her lovely name.

The next day he is gone. Under the relative safety of the early dawn they leave the convent grounds and make for Dunkirk.

The sisters are somewhat disturbed by the presence of a young girl in their midst, and are even more distressed when she appears to have no memory of her past or of who she is. They find Frank's note and this causes a debate as to what to call the silent girl. Lucy, perhaps Francesca? It is an easy decision eventually made by Reverend Mother.

Lucy awakes on her first morning, leaves the little cell of a novice and finds her way to the locked iron gates. For the next three days she watches the remnants pass. Firstly the straggling soldiers of France and Britain mixed in with civilians, who are wondering why they left their farms and villages. They will soon know when they go back to their destroyed fields and buildings, their crops plundered by retreating and advancing armies. Later there are just people, growing fewer and fewer in number, older and older, but still she maintains her vigil. A defeated people are worse to see than a defeated army. She watches until no more people go past and then she watches some more. Now the victorious arrive. She watches as only confident German soldiers march past in impressively strict formations in their long convoys along the road - and they are long. Sometimes, they take hours to pass. They are singing. Then the people begin to pass again, in the opposite direction. They are not singing, but they are at least going home. Her only memories are of the soldier that brought her here. Her only evidence that she existed before are her Rosary Beads, the medal on a ribbon which the sisters tell her is a medal for bravery, and the note the soldier left her. She has been told that she has a family somewhere and that the nuns will do everything they can to trace them.

\*\*\*

Heinz touches the back page of his diary and traces the indentations of words he could have written yesterday. He has not been able to keep up to date with his recording as they have advanced so quickly. They have not really had to engage any British or French soldiers.

They have not seen a living soul for days. They have not really seen that many dead, either. These people appear to be retreating faster than they can march. Maybe the constant need to gather in any fuel and workable artillery has caused them to fall behind. It is not easy to siphon off fuel, particularly diesel, and sometimes the amounts are small. The men will not do it without coffee afterwards to remove the taste. But right at this moment there is no need to stop at all.

"What's the hold up?"

"The Luftwaffe has failed to target the British again, but they have killed a load of civilians."

Commanders are ordered to the front of the single column of tanks and trucks. It takes a few minutes to get there. The engineers are already present, clearing the road of burnt-out vehicles and carts, and the other detritus of explosive warfare. The dead horses are usually most difficult to deal with because of their overall mass. There will be no movement here for at least an hour and there is nothing to scavenge. Heinz decides to forage further forward and in an instant wishes he had not. It looks as though more stray shells and bombs have been used, to devastating effect, about a kilometre further down the road. It is a place where five roads meet and so must have been easy for the advanced troops to bypass the carnage. Everything has been left but many of the dead are now in the field nearby.

Heinz can hear an animal crying and then quickly realises it is a human sound. He takes his sidearm from its leather holster and prepares the gun to fire.

The shattered body of a small boy lies near a dead woman. The boy is crying for his mother and asking for a drink. He is trying to tell his mother that his legs ache from walking all day and that he would like to go home now. It is clear that the small boy is dying. Heinz puts his firearm away and takes out his water flask.

"Mama, where are you? It is very dark."

Heinz walks towards them and places the boy in what is left of his mother's arms, pouring water into what is left of his face. As his life force leaves him the boy can see the wedding photograph of his mother and father. It is the only photograph in the house and it stands quite rightly above the fireplace in their farmhouse. His mother looked very beautiful on her wedding day. He remembers that the soldiers came and burnt his home to the ground and now he can see his mother waving to him through the flames. He feels the enclosing whiteness of her dress and smells her familiar scent. He is pleased to be home and whispers this to her. He likes to be with his mother, she always makes him feel better.

His mother is now talking to someone else. It looks like the lady who lives nearby, and they all join a long line of people. In his pocket he finds his school pencils. He remembers that he has just learned to do joined-up writing. His mother bought them an ice cream on the way home from school when he had shown her his work. Now he knows what he has to do. His turn will come. He realises that as long as his mother is there he will be fine. Everything will be fine.

The boy tries to smile and raise one hand up to his lips as though he is eating his ice cream cone and Heinz lifts his pistol again; it is time to end this agony for both of them. He aims and is about to close his eyes when he is slowly drawn to the stooping figure of a British soldier. He is relieved to be torn away to a scene he understands and expects, but what he sees appals him. This man is stealing from the dead. He is looking around at the ground when he finds something he was looking for. He bends down, puts something in his pocket and reappears with the body of a young girl. She appears to be alive, and covered by a thick black coat. He can no longer fire. He will kill them both as she is protecting his back. The British soldier is now pulling the girl higher so that her legs are on his hips. He leans forward so that the girl will not fall back to the ground and starts to walk down the road. As he turns to look around to see if he has been seen, Heinz has the opportunity to fire but stops when he noticed the Red Cross armband on the soldier's sleeve. He did not come here to kill unarmed medics or young girls. A small swallowing noise makes him look away and see that the boy has died. He is relieved that such a decision has been taken away from him.

He moves the boy so that the mother and her small son are now closer together, and as the young medical soldier moves out of his sight he takes off his own coat and covers their bodies, leaving a note in the pocket of his coat.

The indentations of the words on the page beneath have sensitised his fingers, and, like a blind man reading something over and over, reminds him of what he wrote.

"Is this why we fight?"

He doubts anyone will ever read his message, but he needs to believe that this war is not about little boys and their mothers. He destroys the indented page, a perfect copy of his thoughts.

***

It is a mess. There is only one outcome. They will be captured and then what? There is no organisation. No command structure. Three days of quiet have brought about a sense of false reality. Where are the Germans now? They know that further down the coast at Calais the remaining Allied forces are doing their best to contain the Germans. Last night the sounds of battle started again. To the East the French Army fought the advancing Germans to a standstill. A single order comes that day: Go to the beaches; leave everything, including the wounded. He has no intention of leaving his wounded pilot. He might prove to be his ticket home and he is going home. Even if he is on a plank of wood, he will make it back to England.

He has gone to find food and water for the three of them and arrives at a field hospital to be immediately ordered to assist with the wounded. He tries to explain to the doctor that he has a wounded man but he is safe and needs water and food. The doctor laughs at the silliness of the request but gives him a note - *good luck*, it says. He looks at the doctor and leaves. He has now disobeyed two orders in a day. It makes him feel good because his controlled anger gives him a focus.

A drunken soldier falls past him. He leaves him where he lies. A group of soldiers sways past with a bevy of girls. They are all singing. Well, they are at the seaside. At the top of the beach near the changing cubicles he sees a priest who is holding a service with a small congregation of men. He waits until the holy man blesses them and then asks him for water for an injured man.

"Father," he says. "I have a wounded man. He needs your help."

"Is he dying?"

"No. He just needs water and some food."

The priest laughs but waves him forwards. "Follow me."

Frank realises the priest had no shoes on. "I gave them to a soldier. His need was greater than mine."

He shows him an old-fashioned village fountain and disappears before Frank has chance to thank him. He can see soldiers drinking water from a fountain which is marked *eau non-potable*. It is unsafe and needs boiling. He takes his water bottles from around his neck and fills them with the rank, green water. He receives only abuse when he advises the soldiers about the nature of the water. He trades the last of their cigarettes for some chocolate and corned beef. From a sleeping, drunken soldier he takes half a bottle of cognac. He will not miss it - by morning the man will be in German hands nursing a massive hangover. This is exactly how he will describe it when he arrives home.

There are two types of men on the beach that day, those who want to go home and those that do not think they can make it. He notices as he returns to the relative safety of the dunes that some sort of order is being restored. Officers are marching up and down the beach and placing men from different regiments together. The officers are ready with sidearms and an accompanying professional soldier, usually with stripes; rifles lowered to shooting position are equally at the ready, ready to shoot their own men to restore order. The town has not been sorted but this beach is about to see an old-fashioned sense of discipline. Do as you are told or be shot. The officers are calling for NCOs and each of them are given charge of between ten and fifty men. They are given a ranking soldier who knows what he is to do and so do the other soldiers waiting. Word spreads quickly and men suddenly change from a mob to an army. Each group is given an 'officer in charge', no matter the rank that he was before. Defaulters will pay a price. They are given a time to take their men to a specific place and await further instructions. The beach is suddenly changed from disorder to an orderly group of men with orders to follow - an army again.

A senior officer challenges them with their wounded man. "The orders are to leave the wounded behind."

"This one is coming with us," Frank says. "We have carried him for fifty miles or more, and he is going with us. We'll take care of him. He belongs to us and we are not going without him."

The young officer looks at them. "Right lads, that's what we want to hear. We're not finished yet. The French and our lads are giving them what for near Calais. Good stuff. See you on the other side." He takes something from his pocket and throws it to them - a tin of pilchards.

He gives Frank a small piece of paper. "First out tomorrow, lads. Don't be late or you'll miss breakfast. Winston himself has them making it for you now in Dover. Get yourselves down to the beach."

Frank wonders what he is talking about. He laughs to himself. Pity there are not more officers like this one. This is a man to follow because he knows and understands the nature of human beings. Six small fishes to be shared between them on a day about to become the miracle of miracles; he pours the oily contents of the tin into the mouth of his still unconscious pilot.

\*\*\*

They have reached the beach and walked along the seafront, which is damaged beyond recognition by the presence of thousands of desperate men trying to survive.

In the dunes men are waiting for their turn to come; some are waist deep in the shallows, bobbing up and down like swimmers on a normal summer's day. Small boats are moving to and fro, collecting the silent troops who are devoid of all but their uniforms, and some have less than that. They have carried their wounded man towards the edge of the beach, ignoring instructions to abandon the wounded man on the stretcher. Ignoring the silent, waiting line of men, they wade their way out to a small, approaching fishing boat. It will take fifteen men, no more. The line begins to disperse at the sound of an approaching plane. They take their opportunity to lift the pilot up to the side of the boat as heavy calibre shells begin to rip the water. The wood of the boat splinters as shells pass through its old timbers. As he sinks into the water, the last thing Frank sees is a hole the size of a thumb in his mate's back and a stretcher floating away on the incoming tide.

He sees his sister's grave marked only with her name on a wooden cross that he made himself as he watches his pilot float away on a board of wood that carried him for nearly fifty miles. His mother is smiling at him - and then the sneering face of his father.

"Go on then give in. You always did; too soft. You will never make anything of yourself. I went to Australia when I was your age."

There are many reasons why a young man leaves home at the first opportunity. For the first time Frank wonders why his father had left home just before the Great War broke out.

Salt water stings his eyes and his bleeding hands. The water closes over his head and he is finally at peace. The silence is complete and his journey is over. He just wants to sleep. Again he sees his sister's face and knows his time is over, but a young sailor of a similar age to Frank's sister has other ideas. A boy just out of school, with his father at the boat's helm, doing what hundreds of boys in hundreds of little craft did that day. They pull them out of the water in their thousands, take them home and do not think about who they are. They just take them home. This miracle is not about the fact that the soldiers get home in their hundreds of thousands, and it is not because it appears to be a victory in the jaws of defeat; it is because a whole country can join together and pull off such an event in such circumstances. It says to the watching world, 'We are still here; we are not yet beaten. Come and get us if you can. We will not go quietly.' An old nation that has already lasted for a thousand years forges a new identity this day. And when the doors close on their return, the old nation begins to prepare for whatever is to come.

***

Another man is at peace. The pilot officer long ago accepted that he was going to die. He knew he would never make it back home to Poland. The tide in the Channel pulls him down the coast towards Calais, but the local French people have other ideas. They cannot help at Dunkirk, or at Calais, but between the two great French ports soldiers and sailors and airmen of all shapes and sizes and nationalities are arriving on beaches or being washed ashore. They are removed quickly and quietly to safety and placed in the numerous cellars of farmhouses and barns of small hamlets. The French are going to continue their fight no matter what. They are not going to go quietly, either. For the final time he looks at the sky and realises it is now night. He sleeps. This day a resistance movement is born. It starts to organise the defence of France and it waits. The French, another old nation, know all about waiting.

*** 

Frank awakes to the smell of diesel fumes and vomit. He is covered in oil, much of it in his mouth and ears and even more in his lungs. He coughs but cannot clear the foul smell. A young boy of about fourteen hands him a mug of tea.

"You're lucky," the boy says. "We got you."

There are bullet holes everywhere in the little craft.

"Don't worry," the lad says. "My dad thought of everything." He points at the wheelhouse and shows him the cut up wooden brush handles that are pushed into the holes and held in place by old rags.

"We won't sink. Well, not yet anyway."

Frank passes out. He does not care anymore. He would welcome death right now. He sees faces changing from babies to children to his sister again, smiling and waving to him; a young French girl, with a father's protective arm and his coat around her. It is a shy smile and her wave is an opening and closing of her hand. A small frightened face that is re-assuring him, a grown man of twenty-one. He became of age on the beach this very day. The girl is speaking to him, but she speaks in French, and she is signalling him with a circular motion of her hand. She is telling him to come back.

"He's waking up, dad."

"Right lad, let's have a look at him."

Frank awakens to the sound of voices and two faces above him. They are on the deck of a destroyer. In the far distance he can see the white cliffs that have sent their safe greetings to homecoming travellers to those shores for thousands of years.

"Lost the boat, son; no more trips for us. Guess the wooden blocks did not work so well after all. He did not make it - your mate. I am sorry but he was dead in the water."

"The pilot? The man on the stretcher?"

"He floated away. The strangest thing I ever did see. He just floated away. All that mayhem, pieces of my boat everywhere, and he sailed away like he was on a park lake on a Sunday afternoon. I didn't see him again. What about you?"

"No, dad. Reckon he is dead?"

"Most likely."

Frank makes it to his feet and looks back to where he left his mate, his pilot and an unknown girl. In the distance the French coast shimmers in the man-made heat haze. A town is dying as he watches through oil-stained eyes. The noise of battle can no longer be heard, but there is burning and a plume of smoke rises high to the clouds. Small black dots still swoop along the beaches, dropping their deadly loads. Binoculars would have shown the final men scattering through the dunes looking for cover that is not there. They would have shown a small wooden stretcher being washed ashore much further along the coast. They would have shown a group of French citizens carry the stretcher into the dunes, remove the man's uniform and replace it with their own spare clothes.

The people of Dunkirk have left their homes to burn and gone to the relative safety of the beaches where they had spent many happy summers. They huddle together in the sand dunes and away from the diving planes. Hidden amongst them and in what is left of the nearby town are the tattered remnants of two great armies that have not been rescued by the last of the little boats; a Polish Airman and a young girl with no memory.

\*\*\*

The sisters know something is happening when the Reverend Mother suspends silence at meals for that day. They prayed the previous evening for some good news, and they are not disappointed.

"According to the BBC, a hundred thousand of our soldiers have escaped to England and three hundred thousand British soldiers have escaped too. We should give thanks for this rescue and the gallant sailors and fishermen who risked their lives to overcome such difficulties. You see, sisters, our prayers are answered. We have our miracle - the miracle of Dunkirk."

She looks at the bowed heads, all but one facing the refectory floor. What are they going to do with Lucy? She is gazing into some distant place where all human beings go when there is too much pain to bear. So she goes to the place she visits most. She goes to the gate every day. She is too young to be here. She needs to be with a family.

The Reverend Mother bows her head and prays for one soldier in particular.

\*\*\*

The Polish Airman is firstly aware of feeling very cold and then of how wet he is. He cannot move. The weight of his waterlogged uniform would have been enough but he is also strapped to a hard surface. He tastes salt and can just see the night sky disappearing in and out of the smoke-filled heat haze. He is stranded at the edge of the shore, a piece of flotsam and jetsam like that which arrives on any shore as the tide retreats. He knows the tide has gone out as the beach is quiet; there are no rolling waves. A smell, like that of a match when it ignites, is the only other piece of evidence that tells him that he is still present with the living.

"This one's still alive." A human voice, speaking in a language that he does not comprehend.

"He is lucky."

"Perhaps."

"We need to get him off the beach."

'Remove his uniform too." Female, quiet, assertive.

He is aware of hands on his legs and can now make out the faces of two men and a woman. She has removed his boots. He can feel more hands on his body as the men remove the retaining straps of British Army webbing and what is left of his trousers.

"His legs are injured, quite badly, but there is no bleeding. His wounds are clean and well-cared for. He will need to be carried." Not again. The intense cold of the water, even in June, grips his whole body and he begins to shake uncontrollably, teeth chattering, eyes unfocussed. They put a coat over him, covering his near nakedness.

"Anything of value?"

"No."

He feels a round metal object in his mouth and for the first time, fear. The burning sensation in his mouth floods his body with relief and a warmth that he recognises.

"Easy with that stuff." A jealous male voice.

"He is a pilot."

"A lousy one; he is on the ground."

"What do we do with him?"

"Bring him to my place."

"Typical of you, Elizabeth."

"What do you mean? Be quiet. You are not my father."

"No, I am your brother, and that is not what I meant. It is too dangerous. Where would you hide him?"

"He can stay in what is left of the pigeon loft."

"As you wish. Now we move." An older, even more assertive male voice.

They walk along the shore to an open land drain, follow it back under the beach road and find their way to a track into a small wood. While her two brothers form a chair with their arms to carry him he is unaware that she is studying him carefully. She found his identity tags and some papers in his pocket and recognises the uniform of a fellow countryman. It will be a problem finding papers for him but that will keep for a few days. There are many displaced people all over France, many of whom are still going south towards Spain or Switzerland and the French Ports.

\*\*\*

He wakes up. He hurts all over; he knows he is tired but still alive. A force surges through his body. It is a sensation similar to flying. He has recovered. His body tells him that it is well but still in recovery. He remembers feeling this way as a small child after illness. He opens his eyes but his mother is not there. He closes them as he feels the ebbing pain of his legs taking over his feelings. They ache badly and he is suddenly aware of everything that has passed, but is unaware of how long he has been asleep. His legs are wrapped in clean bandages and his head feels like he has been drinking his father's cherry vodka. He checks his body as he would the flight controls. Everything is present; there is nothing missing, but he is aware of something he cannot quite put his mind to. The conscious mind is asserting itself. It needs to measure how the body is, whether it would support life or not. His eyes focus on a figure at the window. He knows neither the figure nor the window. The light through the shuttered window shows it is still daytime and that the figure is female. She is looking through the small gap offered by the shutters.

"What do you see?"

"France." He is amazed when she replies in Polish.

"Where in France?"

"Picardy."

"And where is that?"

"The North."

"And what do you see?"

"A beautiful day in a French village full of German soldiers."

"And where are we?"

"Right in the middle of them."

In his state of pleasant exhaustion his legs give way and he falls into her strong arms. He is surprised that she can hold him.

"I was a nurse."

"A strong one."

"It's all in the technique."

"Did you find me?"

"I was there."

"Who are you?"

"A friend."

"Do you have a name?"

"Not yet."

"Where are the rest of my clothes?"

"Gone."

"They are that bad?"

"The smell was rather awful, but we destroyed your uniform to protect you. They are everywhere."

"Who are everywhere?"

"The Germans. They are searching for survivors. We would all probably be shot if they found you."

"I don't remember you taking my clothes off. And this is not mine."

She smiles at his long gown. "No, it's not yours, and no, I did not actually undress you. But you did not want to be clean. You fought us every moment of the way. Madame Lefebvre finally stripped you completely. No one argues with Madame. Not even me. When did you last change your underclothes?"

"Do not know. Do not remember. What day is it today? Weeks ago."

"It smelled like it was months."

"Probably."

"I prefer clean men."

"So do I."

"Funny."

"Really."

"Open the shutters."

"Too dangerous."

"Open them."

"Why?"

"I need to see you."

"Why?"

"So that I know I am alive and not in the presence of an angel."

"You are alive and I am no angel."

"I need to see and know."

She opens the window and stands back to see the sharp light of what can only be a June day in France.

"Before you ask, I am Polish."

"How long have you been in France?"

"I was born here."

"Does that not make you French?"

"Not necessarily."

"Your parents are Polish refugees?"

"Yes. Now stop looking at me."

"How could any man not wish to look at you?"

She is in shadow now but he recognises the high cheekbones, features that define his countrywomen. He sees the long fingers that shaved him - and not just his face. He realises what he missed during the physical inventory. He has been completely shaved, head to foot. He rubs the slight stubble on his head.

"You were very hairy, especially your legs."

"Thank you."

"Madame Lefebvre insists that to treat wounds you must be shaved everywhere. She will not do the shaving for her young men however."

"I notice you were very careful. Nothing missing."

She looks at him.

"Just who is this Madame Lefebvre?"

"She is eighty years old and thinks you are a little boy."

"A little boy named Toni."

"Elizabeth."

"Lizzie."

"No. I only answer to Elizabeth."

"Pardon. Lizzie is my sister's name."

"I am not your sister."

"Clearly."

He continues to watch the tall, graceful young woman who continues to watch the scene in the village. Her view is unclear through the ancient glass but the room is full of light and warmth.

"What do you see?"

"They are leaving."

"So it's over?"

"No, our fight has only just begun." She misunderstands his question. "We are already organising our people. They are angry at being beaten and will not take this lying down. You know the British pulled off an amazing feat. They evacuated their entire army across the Channel. Many French soldiers are in England right now, too."

"England will fall. These people cannot be stopped."

"Maybe, but the Germans will work out the cost of invading England, and then there is the cost of taking Scotland, Wales and Ireland. They will not take it lying down, either. That is what we must do here. We have to make them think that it is pointless as long as we are not totally defeated. They cannot occupy the whole of France and then invade England. They do not have enough men. We need to keep them busy. As long as the British are free then we have a chance too. The Germans will not be willing to sacrifice the numbers of men that would be required to beat them."

"My last memory is of being on that beach with the soldiers." He is trying to remember if he knows the names of the soldiers who carried him. "How did I get here?"

"We carried you."

"Is this before or after you stole my clothes?"

"If you must know, we took your uniform off straight away. For one thing it was soaking wet, and if we were caught carrying a soldier things would have been difficult."

"Airman."

"If we were caught carrying an airman we would have been shot. And of course you were filthy."

"Did you save any of my clothes?"

"No." She nods to a pile of clothes at the foot of the makeshift bed. "You are welcome to try those. They belonged to my brothers."

She turns her back to allow him to dress and she giggles as she catches sight of his naked rear in the mirror. He will do, she thinks, as she sees the broad shoulders disappearing beneath an old work shirt to be tucked in with a belt holding loose, over-sized trousers and socks that are also too big.

"Where are your brothers?" Toni half-expects them to arrive and find him with their sister. He fancies that might be as bad as the Germans finding him.

"My brothers are further south. They are watching the Germans to see what they are planning."

"They are planning to occupy France, but they may not be able to hold all of it."

"Further south? How far have the Germans reached?"

"They are already in Paris. Some are in Bordeaux. The French Government are suing for an armistice. The fighting is mainly over." Elizabeth had heard one of the last news bulletins.

"What is the date?"

"It is the fourteenth of June."

"What year?"

"Don't be silly."

"I cannot remember the last time I had anything to eat."

"Wait."

She starts to feed him some thick soup. "We need to get you well enough to get you to England. We assume you did not steal the pilot officer's uniform."

"Why, are you impressed by men in uniform?"

"Only if they belong in them."

"Then no, I did not steal the uniform and I am not going to England unless you come with me." He reaches out as if to touch her face.

She smiles and allows the soup to run over his lips. "You are drooling," she says in retribution and pretend rejection.

\*\*\*

It is the last moment for Heinz to know of the taste of victory as he stands on a very broad, sandy shore and looks out across the Channel towards England. It is a very pleasant, warm June day. He knows that the gently sloping beach should be filled with local people seeking the fresh air and pleasantness that only the sea and a beach can bring. There should be families here with their children, playing and eating together, as would be normal on any June day by the sea side in France or anywhere else. There should be grandfathers holding their children's children in the shallows of the water, letting them kick and splash, allowing them the first experience of the feel of a great ocean of water; naked babies in the warm shallows feeling the particles of sand slide between their feet and bottoms, feeling safe and secure in the strong hands that would not allow them to come to harm. There should be grandmothers telling their daughters to cover their babies' heads and keep them in the shade, even if granddad has just taken them to the water's edge.

"What is your father doing allowing the baby to sit in the water and she just over a cold? Did you have her chest examined by the doctor yet?"

They try to pass on a lifetime of experience without interfering with the parents' wishes. Parents once again eye each other as lovers as when they first met. They are still in love and a set of grandparents is giving them a little time to themselves before they return to the routine of their lives.

"Why don't you two go for a walk? Have sometime for yourselves. Have a coffee, or a beer. We will watch the baby."

They want some time with their grandchildren too. They need to prove that they are still useful and know how to help babies to grow. They know they must not interfere and advice is carefully given. This is an especially precious time for them and they want to experience it as best they can. They know that their time is limited by their age. For them, holding a small, breathing human being is the greatest joy they have left to experience. In some ways it is better than when they had their own children. They do not want to feed them or clean them; they just want to know that they are alive through them and will continue to be in the future. This is why they are so important to grandparents. This is why grandparents are so important to them.

This beach should be covered in picnic blankets, buckets and spades and towels, and umbrellas, and sand castles, and human beings having a good time, maybe thinking about their futures, or reflecting on their pasts, perhaps planning the week ahead. Perhaps trying to figure out how to apologise to each other for some indiscretion, or maybe making love at night because the baby will be in the grandparents' house because it is their wedding anniversary and they are babysitting. It should be full of young men and women learning how to approach each other and take friendships to a higher level. It should have young girls with boys staring at them, but not knowing what to say. Young men who for the first time start to look at girls in a different way. Young women who talk to each other about what they want in a man, and young men who know what they want from a woman - two completely different things. One is philosophical the other biological. Somehow they manage to accommodate both for each other. The heat of the sun, the gentle breeze and the sound of water takes humanity back to a simple age of primitive survival, when life is not complicated except by the need to continue to survive.

"So what has changed?" he thinks out loud.

But this beach is strewn with a number of the dead, and the debris of the people who did not survive, who have just lost a war and who have left quickly. The tide is in full flow and the flotsam and jetsam of the sea is being washed to and fro. There are still bodies in the water and they are slowly being rolled by the tide, giving them the eerie appearance of life. Some of them collide at the water's edge, like young men do on a summer's day out, cavorting in the foaming water trying to outdo each other for their friends to see, or maybe to compete for the favours of a chosen girl. But this beach is deserted of the living now, save for the few who do the worst job of all. They remove the unexploded munitions and weapons left behind. Another, separate group, often as a punishment, remove the dead, but the fact is that there are not that many dead. Perhaps previous tides have taken the dead out to sea, but he doubts that. The soldiers know that their enemies have largely been repatriated. Perhaps there are not that many dead?

This recovery group is supervised closely. They are the lowest of the low; personal effects are supposed to be handed over to the senior officers, not just for intelligence gathering but because the Red Cross will be informed of the known dead. He notices one of them about to pocket a dead soldier's belongings. He raises his hand and snaps his fingers at the man, who brings him a gold wedding ring, a watch and a wallet, and the soldier's identity tags. He opens the wallet to find a letter and a photograph of two little girls who no longer have a father. He looks at the letter and knows it is from the man's wife. He looks at the beach scavenger and places the belongings in his own pocket.

"Unlike you, he was not scum. He died with honour, defending his country. You are not worthy of such a man. I do not know which prison you have come from, but if I discover you doing this again I will personally shoot you and later, when you ask me to, I will kill you." He walks to the corpse of his enemy and returns his identity to him, and then walks up the beach and hands the other items to an officer that he outranks.

"When this is over I shall check that this man's wife has received all of his personal belongings."

The officer notes the Waffen SS insignia on his collar.

"Understand?"

"Yes, Sir."

Finally, death has touched him directly and he is shocked by his response to handing over the belongings of the dead soldier. He reaches the top of the beach and steps over the low sea wall. The town is dead too - destroyed. Yet next to the beach, a fountain of water still splashes into a shallow pool, with a warning sign that the faintly green water is not to be used for drinking; it is surrounded by dead British soldiers. The pools of blood mingle with water and the torn uniforms indicate that it was not the water that killed them. He sees one man with no boots and realises that he was a man of God, as he wears the collar of a chaplain. He is sad to find communion hosts in his pockets. He does not know what faith the priest was but he eats them anyway. The same officer is still nearby. He calls him over and demands an explanation as to why these men are still by the fountain. The officer explains to him that the orders are to clear the beaches first and make them safe, and then work into the town. He looks at the officer, who is clearly unhappy at his current duties.

"Why have you ended up doing this?"

"I refused to fire upon women and children who were sheltering in a church."

"You were fortunate not to be shot."

"Yes, maybe I would have been, but moments later the church was hit by a shell and the order was no longer relevant. My commanding officer was killed by the same shell from our own guns. I gave the order to advance, but one of the junior officers still reported me and so here I am pending further enquiries."

Heinz stops him from talking further. He takes out his small black book and lead pencil from his pocket. He begins to write an order, an unusual event in itself, but it looks like a simple direction. 'The church is full of women and children. Take account of this as you advance further.' He signs his name, crumples up the paper and drops it into the mud by the fountain. He picks it up and gives it to the officer. It is just legible.

"Now, you have your excuse, but I want this mess tidied up first. There is a chaplain amongst the dead here and he deserves to be treated well. I want the names and ranks of all the others noted and any useful information sent to the intelligence people. But you - you are to make sure that everyone you find here is duly recorded and dealt with according to their rights. I have given you reason to find a future and I expect you to return my kindness in full."

He receives a nod and knows his real order would be carried out to the letter.

"By the way, where are all the townsfolk? Surely they are not all dead."

"I do not know, but look." He points towards a small building, which appears intact. It is flying a red cross. "Perhaps they are all hiding there."

The people have mainly dispersed back to the countryside and other beaches, which have dunes. He wonders where all those people who had been walking towards the town have gone. He thought the town would be full, and therefore full of the dead. Where is the famous British Army, where has the great French Army gone? Why are they themselves held back? It is almost an empty victory. They got away. But killing is not the objective. They are building a greater Europe. Where would they have put 350 000 prisoners of war? How would they have fed them? No, it was logical to allow them to escape. As a fighting force the British have nothing left. If they invade England now it will be simple.

A little voice cautions his euphoria. *Are you so sure?* They would be defending their own country this time, and England does not have the flat, open countryside and roads of France. And before they could conquer England, once they got there, there would the matter of London. They would have to go around it first. Its river has no crossings to the East and only congested, easily destroyed ones in the centre - and they would be destroyed.

They have a bridge that can be left in the 'up' position and defended. Unlike the French with Paris, the English would willingly sacrifice London and Birmingham and then perhaps even Manchester and they would still be 200 miles from the Scottish Border. How many dead Germans soldiers would that mean? The Western cities and even the smaller coastal villages and ports could be supplied by the largest navy in the world and that might force the Americans to join in too, as the anti-British Ireland would be drawn into the conflict. He even imagines Ireland being taken again by the English. Certainly, Ireland would experience a massive influx of population as ex-pats return from England. Then whose side would the Americans fight on? England could easily remove its navy and air force to Northern Ireland and continue its fight from there. Its Empire would furnish the rest. The Welsh and the Scots are notorious for the defence of their lands. They might put up with their neighbours and fight with them occasionally, but defer to the Germans? Not likely, not ever. His mind races away with his thoughts as he gazes across the calm water to the hazy coastline of England.

He realises that taking the British island is not the same as pouring troops down through Belgium or Holland and across a massive front line where you can best pick a fight that you know you can win. The French had had their Maginot line but it meant nothing. They simply went past it. They had not even attacked it in any numbers. It was still intact and manned when France fell. He forces his mind to think positively and calmly.

He thinks about taking a souvenir but rejects the idea as immoral. It will make him as bad as the scum on the beach. It is not for him. Why would you want a dead man's watch, or even his cap badge? Their side arms are not as attractive as his own, and not as deadly. He has no objective except to be a good soldier - that is enough. It is reward enough. He wants his family to be proud of him, especially his wife. He wishes that she was here with him, his slender girl with long, dark, braided hair that ends halfway down her back. She wore her hair like that on their wedding day and when she first came to him in their bed. He had never seen her like that before, with her face open to show truly its simple beauty, and to be reminded of a woman with a very clear way of thinking. How could you put all of that into one human being? It was then he realised that he would always have to share her with the rest of the world, everybody and every man. They all saw what he knew. But she had chosen him and that makes him feel special. He selects a smooth, soft, white pebble as his souvenir of his visit to this beach.

*** 

Soon after their first times together, she speaks carefully to him, trying to lead him into the world of responsibility. He has gone home from the now deserted beach with a simple souvenir of a pebble with a very definite shape and pattern taken from the place of final victory, and as she lies in his arms after they have been as close as a man and woman can be she speaks to him.

"You own my spirit," she concedes.

"As you do mine."

"No. Not quite. Not really. You left something inside me and I cannot do the same for you. That makes a difference and so it makes it special."

"What have I left inside you?"

"What does a man normally leave inside a woman after they have been this close?"

"That does not mean I own you, or you me."

"Do remember how you meant to propose to me?"

"How could I forget?"

"Well you have achieved your wish. We are expecting our first child. So you own me and I own you until our child is born. That is what we agreed."

It is all he can do to smile in contentment, and shake his head in wonderment. He moves closer to her and smells the slight dampness of her hair. He kisses her neck and places his hands to caress her in the place where he imagines their child is. He holds her close; she is protected by his love and his body.

She is pleased at his reaction. She sleeps. He packs quietly; leave is always just too short, especially for a soldier. When she wakes in the morning he has gone. He leaves a short note expressing his love for her and their unborn child. She saves his words until later in the day and is pleased with his choice of telling her how he feels about her and their future together. She imagines him whispering the words to her just as she is about to sleep. Her mother told her to marry a good man. She would have been pleased with her choice. When she wakes in the morning his message is still in her hand but she has to leave it quickly as the changes in her body are making her feel nauseated - or is it the sea-smelling pebble left on the table next to her bed?

***

He is itching everywhere. He relies on others to pick out his clothes. They chose his most comfortable clothes too, so that this would not happen - a white cotton shirt and light brown jacket. It may be warm in Paris, he has been informed, but for him it is the trenches again. He did not think that particular vile monster would rear its ugly head again. This has been too easy. In his wildest dreams he could not have imagined it. He has just defeated two of the greatest armies in the world. He has; no one else. He thinks how other great men must have felt at their moment of glory. Did they itch? Did they have nightmares? Being buried alive really only became part of warfare in the trenches. He needs to go home. He needs the security of his familiar places. He needs to know that he will never be buried alive.

Beneath his gaze from the Jardins de Trocadero the people of Paris are already returning to their normal activities. He wonders if they ever changed; beautiful young women in their finest clothes, walking with a sense of purpose through the parks and gardens of this city, which he now owns. Children playing with their mothers on the green lawns still vibrant from the early summer, not yet parched by the strong sun, unaware that they are now his conquered people. He allows a sense of pride to enter his feelings. They are not of pure stock, but they have their own individualism. They look normal. He looks at the Tower. It is unpleasant and will have to be removed eventually. It is not natural. It should be made of natural stone if it is to be acclaimed as truly beautiful. The concrete wall to his front gives him some protection as he feels faint from looking at the steep drop before him. He does not want anyone near him. He wants this moment to himself. He feels complete, like a newly married man with a beautiful new wife, but his gaze in time will soon turn. He will go home to make his next plan. He knows he will not return here and so allows his private photographer to complete the pictures before taking one last look at the Tower. He will have it destroyed. It gives him no pleasure. It is ugly; and now it is his to do with as he pleases, like most of Europe and its peoples.

The children are settling down in the park to have their lunches. Summer will soon be over and Paris will be like any other capital city in winter. The mothers of Paris take note, say nothing and do not watch his greatest moment. They are aware, but not watching. The corner of an eye is sometimes enough. It is enough to know that many of their husbands, brothers and fathers made it back to their families, back to their jobs. They will go about their lives in the usual way and wait this out. It is stamped in the very soul of these people of this land. We can wait and we will.

As a gesture he laughs a few times and points to various areas of the city from his view point. Perspiration runs down his back. The itching becomes worse, especially near the scar tissue in his rear end. He takes one final look at the gardens, the smart women and the well-fed children. He purses his lips and nods in the way that his entourage now know means he has had enough and it is time to go, like a small child who wishes to move on to the next toy, so they leave.

From the corner of the eye that only women seem to have they note that he has gone from his point of observation. They relax and smile at their children. They are all thinking exactly the same thing. Why should they not? Firstly, they are all French, and they are all very capable of making a judgement about a man on sight. They have been trained well by their older sisters, mothers and grandmothers.

'Small,' they all think. 'He is very small.'

Then they do something which women from time immemorial have done. They look at each other and realise that they are perhaps in a dress that is no longer fashionable; their shoes are a little scuffed, but the young girl over there has a very pretty dress and her hat is so *now*. Just wait until she has her first baby. She will not be so pert then. No time to smoke and drink coffee with her lover. They pack away their picnics and put their babies into their prams. They tidy themselves and their make-up; their husbands will be home soon. If the weather lasts they will be back here tomorrow, perhaps in a new dress, purchased by their grateful lovers before a new anything becomes a thing of the past. Then they leave the park and go home; and he has been dismissed.

***

Hannah watches as her trees move in the strong wind. The trees have always been here in her park. They are as old as the square itself. It defines her city and the people who live there. The trees are hundreds of years old. She cannot put her arms around them. When she walked with Heinz they had just managed to touch hands when they both embraced their magnificent circumferences. The trees have been witness to many things in this great city. Trees are part of all cities, which never look quite right without their lakes, parks and trees; they provide a sense of belonging or ownership. It is the connection human beings have with their ancestral past; her grandfather had explained to her when she was a little girl. He had explained to her how the first human beings had trekked across continents looking for food, water and shelter. When caves were not available humans turned to the trees to give them shelter in simple structures. The trees still provide a resource for human beings and they hold a record of every event that took place in their environment as their rings grow and increase every season that passes.

Hannah's trees and their leaves have just reached their first full colours of spring. They have lost the first freshness of their leaves but still have some time to go before the first call of autumn when the cold will shock them into shedding their leaves. The spring light forces the colours to glimmer in the early morning light. The life within her is new too. Her spirit has been awakened by the small body within her. She feels whole; their love for each other has produced this child. She walks to the bench where she first sat with her husband. Who had kissed who first? Something folded within her makes her move without reason. She holds the edge of the bench.

"Your first?" A lady had sits down next to her, making a note of the small bump. Hannah nods. She really wants to be alone with her unborn child. She does not want to be rude.

"I could not have children. People do not understand that these days. You are supposed to have lots of healthy children. I hope you do."

Hannah smiles at her. "One will be enough for now."

She takes out her knitting. "I will make something for the baby - in white so it does not matter if it is a boy or a girl. What would you like? When is the baby due? Winter? A hat, a cardigan, leggings and mittens; I will make them all. I sit here every day about lunchtime and watch the river while I knit or sew. Sometimes I even read a book, but you have to be careful these days what you are seen reading. My name is Helena."

"Hannah."

"A Jewish name?"

"Perhaps, but I have a name my father chose for me because he liked it."

"If you are a Jewess you should leave the country now and have your baby in a place at peace with itself."

"Why?"

"It is dangerous here for some people. You and your husband should consider America - a good life there, they say, plenty of work and land. People are still leaving. Perhaps I could help you?" She looks around to see if anyone has heard their brief exchange of words.

"I must go. I will be here every day."

"Nice to have spoken with you."

"Perhaps socks first I think. That's what the soldiers always ask for."

Hannah returns to the riverside bench every day at the same time. As part of her birth preparations as she tries to keep herself fit. On the seventh day she sees a small parcel beneath the bench with her name on it. Long winter socks for a small baby. Each week there is a small gift from her benefactor and then a final note with a winter hat. 'If ever you need me, return an item of clothing and leave me a message.'

Hannah's sole aim is to be a good mother. She wants to have the perfect child and believes this will happen with the perfect pregnancy. She works out that early human beings ate lots of fruit and vegetables with little or no fat and no alcohol or cigarettes. This is a good thing, she thinks. She plans a simple diet. Her doctor is worried because she does not put on a lot of weight and yet he sees a very healthy young woman with a very healthy baby inside her. It has the strongest heartbeat he has ever heard and when he places the stethoscope on the growing bulge a quick response followed. The baby kicks back straight away. It does not like the cold. A girl, he thinks, believing in one of his many personal but unvalidated theories.

*** 

The wireless waits for the warmth of its valves to increase before it can interpret the fast-as-light signals to cover its circuits and turn them into sound. A hum of irrelevant incandescent electrons buzz through the glass-sealed vacuums that separate the two meanings of signal and sound for at least one minute. Amplification of sound starts with a crackle and a hiss as words travel across the ethereal spaces between sender and receiver. Old words take on new meanings as the radio became the first such item to occupy the home. The very name itself - the wireless - indicated it did not require a wire like the telephone or telegraph. But its capability has to wait until the arriving energy is moved and amplified; a long time when you are waiting for the *News of the Day*, when your son is part of a defeated army, when he should have been home long ago if he is still alive. His name is barely mentioned in their household. It hangs in the air like a slow-falling parachute, carrying information but never landing, a trance-like state that induces a constant questioning in the mind of Frank's mother. She has stopped asking her husband about 'what if' and 'why do we not know?' He is a terse man with no response to anything. He can offer no consolation. He is not capable. He keeps repeating the same statement about waiting to receive a telegram and that he will answer her when it arrives; everyone and everything annoys him. His son did not need to go to war, even to serve as a medical orderly. He had found his son a good job on the railways, a reserved occupation - no war for his sons if he could help it. They were not going to die for King and country, not if he could do something about it. The only thing he was going to volunteer for was the extra money to be earned by taking on training, which also meant a posting away from home; soldiers are not the only conscripts in this war.

The radio finally settles down to its working temperature and a voice indicates the start of the news on the BBC Home Service. It reveals that the last men have been taken off the beach at Dunkirk and that three days before the captain of a destroyer was taken ashore in the dark. He walked up and down the beach shouting to see if anyone had been left behind from the final assembly points. The sailors waited anxiously in the motor boat for one hour before believing they had completed their mission then they, too, went home. They all spoke later of the eerie silence of the place, which had been something of a safe haven for a destroyed army that now held out some possibility of a future. They were all to be commended for their bravery.

Outside the house a man surveys the fading terrace of small homes with big families and thinks briefly about his reception. Knowing his father is at work helps him to knock at the door. The lady of the house recognises the knock and a sound like cutlery falling on the tiled floor echoes through the relative silence of the empty home. He can just hear a man's voice on the radio as the door opens to reveal his mother in her usual apron with duster in hand. And she sees the torn figure of her son, she takes hold of his hands and leads him to the small living room; her son is home. She nods to herself, thinking immediately of all the other mothers who will never have this experience of relief.

"Frank, Frank, sit down. Let me make you some tea." She bustles around the table, fussing over the clean linen and setting places for the whole family.

"There is only you and me, mam."

She starts to cut the freshly made bread. She trembles. She looks at him again. 'Is he really here?' The silent question forms within her mind.

"You never could cut it straight, mam. Let me." He reaches to take the knife but she leaves the knife on the old bread board and falls into his arms and stays there until her sobs subside.

"Sit," she says as she disappears for a moment into the kitchen. He cuts the last of the bread as the last of the sand falls through the clear, glass-shaped dumbbells drawn down by gravity - a device that fascinated him as a little boy and still causes him to gaze at such a simple and yet such an accurate measurement of time.

"Eggs are ready, mam."

She has never learned not to fuss, a habit caused by her particular husband, who has high expectations of everyone else but himself. She watches him eat slowly, methodically, one hand stretched out as if protecting his food. She notes the slight tremble as he lifts the cup of tea to his mouth. Even with milk from a tin it is the best drink he has ever had. She notices the oil-stained uniform and the dirt ingrained in his skin. Clothes beyond redemption, a body that can be repaired but eyes that tell a different story. Her brother had come back from the last war with those eyes. He had never been whole again.

"Look at your clothes, son. Look at you. What happened?"

"Mam, some of the lads came back with no clothes on at all. If it wasn't for the folks of Dover we would all be filthy and naked. They came with the clothes of their husbands, brothers and sons and food they could not afford - clothes that are not even spares. All I have is my boots and tunic, everything else was given to me. It was beyond description. We all had to be checked. They thought there might be Germans mixed in with us and there probably were. I had to assist with the wounded until they were cleared. They would not let any of us tell anyone we were safe."

"Well you are now, son."

"Yes, mam."

"I'll put some water on for a bath for you."

"No, mam, I need to sleep."

Time passes and he recognises the familiar sounds of the house. His clothes disappear and people come and go and look in on him. He sleeps.

He hears his mother say to the visitors, "Our Frank is home."

\*\*\*

In the late summer sunshine Frank watches his two younger brothers being lifted onto the train by their mother. Carefully written luggage labels and sweets cannot cover the emotion of those departures. He remembers his own pain and sees it in his mother's eyes. An ache caused by a small, vindictive man who is on the verge of destroying a continent. They return to their now empty house, a hive of activity just two hours before and now worse than a morgue. He thinks of the pain shared with another family in France. A daughter believed to be dead left behind at some unmarked crossroads. He wonders if they had been able to return to try to find her.

His mother is winding up string and putting cardboard luggage labels into her sewing box. 'Safe for now,' she is thinking. The news on the radio is reflective of the apprehension in country.

"More rumours of the invasion." She switches off the radio.

"Listen." The silence of a warm summer's evening carries through the open windows. There are no voices in the street. No late cricket matches, no shouts calling time for bed. Childhood stolen away by the same, small man.

"I hope their children are in the countryside too. I don't want any German mothers to feel the same way as I do."

"Mum, they will be back soon." Most of them are nearby in the countryside.

It is the women's faces that keep coming back to him. They had said goodbye to their older sons and husbands as they went off to France. They had waited for their return and now they had said goodbye to their babies. Small hands holding even smaller hands. Identical instructions across a whole country given by mothers holding in their emotions:

"Stay together. Keep your brother with you. Don't get separated. Send your card when you arrive." Twelve-year-olds became mothers and fathers overnight, too frightened to be homesick, but homesick nonetheless. Husbands hold their wives close that night and pretend to be unaffected. They too, although playing the role of men, are close to the edge. They should have been playing cricket in the streets with their boys or rounders with their girls.

"So tell me again about the young girl in France. The one you saved."

He thinks about saying no, as he doesn't want to talk about it, but knows it will now be pointless to refuse. His mother would have made a good detective. "She is like our Lucy, mam. You know; curls and a lovely smile. She saved me, mam."

"You saved her, son," his mother says with obvious pride. "People should know."

"No, mam. I may have not really helped her at all. I think her family thought she was dead. They may be dead too."

"A day will come when she will return to her loved ones. You have to believe that. When we are all together again."

"And if they are dead?"

"She will have you and us if needs be. You could try to contact the convent through the church."

"Yes, mam. I know. I will."

***

From the attic window Frank can see the small garden. Lucy's swing has finally fallen apart and its ropes hang limply from the tree branch. He finds it hard to believe that it is still early summer and the final stems of daffodils are still present beneath the tree line. In the corner is an Anderson shelter, partly built by his father, ignoring the instructions and giving up, as he did on everything he did. This shelter offers no protection. A strong wind could blow it over. A direct hit by a bomb still offers no protection.

Frank and his mother remove the corrugated galvanised structure and he begins to dig the hole necessary to anchor the structure.

In the failing light Frank continues to read the instructions for the shelter. He will complete its construction tomorrow. He needs something to occupy his mind. It is lights out now and blackout curtains. His bedroom window provides the knowledge that small fires are being lit in the fields. They grow in size hoping to attract the pathfinder bombers with their incendiary bombs attracting them away from their city target. The attack is coming. Small explosions out in the fields indicate that he is right. Where is the warning? He can hear the ships at the docks sounding their klaxons taken up by the crescendo of the city's air raid warning system. Across the city, sand-filled buckets are being thrown onto the small, sparkling devices that can melt metal and destroy the binding forces of concrete and mortar. The heat of the chemical reaction is offered no resistance. The sand is able to combine the materials and turn them into glass.

His mother has made a space for him under the stout kitchen table. She has nailed a thick blanket to the far end of the table nearest the brown papered windows. He settles down for the night, noticing his mother flinch with every shattering blow that takes the city apart, brick by brick, stone by stone, levelling shops and factories, indiscriminate, unaware of the cost of human life. Those who survive the onslaught on the ground will wake tomorrow to a very different world with unfamiliar streets, scarred buildings and landscapes and faces of unrecognisable people.

At 9.35 p.m. the windows of their small house are blown in. The searing heat passes across his face like a brick kiln venting itself into a workshop. He thinks he is covering them both with the thick blanket, waiting for the next blast that does not come. The sticky brown paper has done its job holding shards of glass in position, as has the table, which has not moved, unlike his mother, who went at the first chance. She is already outside. She is not going to be buried alive. He runs to the destroyed front door only for his mother to appear at the back door. Outside it is snowing dust already. The house opposite has taken a direct hit. He runs towards the house and is stopped by pieces of plaster and brick that are now falling everywhere. He has left without his tin hat. He turns to run back as his mother appears at the front door. He has never seen her without her hair up or covered with a hat or scarf. He is astonished to know his mother has waist long hair with a slight hint of red. So that is where his beard colour comes from. And under all those layers of clothes and aprons she is a very dainty lady. And there she is with the very hat.

"Go quickly," she says. "There are children in that house. They were not all evacuated."

The next morning they carry away the bodies of seven young children. Frank did his best but he could only assist the living. The Air Raid Warden is blowing his stack.

"This is why we use shelters. We do not stay in buildings. Where are the bloody parents?"

Frank had known this family all of his life. He remembers the birth of the younger children with ease. Two of the children had been with the parents looking for relatives to shelter them from the storm. They had gone to a nearby village without telling anyone and the twelve-year-old daughter had been left in charge. The parents return a few hours later to place a small posy of flowers on what is left of the steps of the building. Frank never sees them again, they just became part of the displaced and forgotten, but he does retrieve the card when the seven small roses have withered. There is just one other word on it: *Sorry.*

As he tucks the card into his pocket his mother asks him to go and find his dad. He was due back that morning.

\*\*\*

Sterling silver arrows of bright aluminium flick and flak across the blue skies of high summer; Frank does not know how to estimate the heights of these planes. They are closer to the edge of space than any other human beings have ever been. They are the Spitfires and Hurricanes of the RAF, but are being flown by experienced pilots of other countries. A rag tag and bobtail of a squadron that was not considered good enough to fly with the RAF.

The Poles, in particular, have already learnt how to fly in the heat of battle. They fly without fear and their enemies are aware of them above all others because they fly with hatred. They not only expect to die for their beloved homeland but they almost appear to welcome it. They are good pilots with their own effective tactics and they are well-trained. They are the misfits of the RAF and have no desire to conform. They never will. They have much to offer the beleaguered RAF, which is close to an unacknowledged defeat.

There are no defenders left on the ground as someone in either desperation or necessity has given permission for them to join the fight, and they are wreaking havoc. Frank watches them fly straight at the German planes, which try to stay in their strict formations. They have not yet fired their weapons but are forcing their opponents to separate out to avoid collision with them, and like birds of prey they wait and circle the outriders who have left the flock and take them out. He wonders if his pilot from the stretcher is in the battle, but doubts it.

German planes of all types are now falling from the sky in large numbers. The bombers are not making it to their targets as their own defenders are fought off, or run out of fuel, or luck. Red hot engine fumes condense rapidly in the coolness of the high sky and become visible against the blue as vapour trails criss-cross to form a portcullis shielding the homes and people below. These high flyers have only the problem of defence to think about. They are close to home. They are defending their castle. They do not have to take the attack anywhere else; it is coming here, right on their doorstep, in their territory. They are waving them in like a cook shouting to them to come and get the food. Lunch is served. We are here. We are waiting for you. They can land and quickly re-arm and refuel. The pilots shift restlessly from foot to foot as if this will hurry up the mechanics, but they take their time. These are their machines and they want them to return. The pilots and their battle will have wait until they have checked oil and fuel. It is their part and they play it well. The armourers feel the machine gun bullets leave their planes as they watch from below and know that if one makes it to a target then they have completed their part in the mission. They have played their part in full measure. They and the pilots are consoled by the thought that they did not cause this. It is not of their making. These are the thoughts that will see them through the worst part of their work, when the dead come marching home in their thousands. These, too, are the thoughts of the thousands sheltering below, praying and hoping that what looks like too few small aeroplanes will defend their country.

The noise of the battle is too high to register at ground level and Frank's concentration is brought to the sound of voices raised in anger. He observes an event which he will recall for the rest of his life. Not every pilot is in the sky. A large, red-headed man is pulling at his similarly coloured beard and jumping up and down on the wing of a Spitfire. The mechanic has been unable to start the plane. A comic scene perhaps, but the rage of the pilot-in-waiting is all the more pointed as his Polish brothers in the sky are starting to get the upper hand. An anger, cold and calculated, and all the more pointed, is aimed upwards, as he never takes his eyes off the sky. He feels he is being denied his opportunity to seek revenge. He has no intention of losing two countries to these despicable people with the black crosses on their wings.

Finally, the engine roars into life and with toolbox, spanners, nuts and bolts, and a man in blue overalls falling off a wing, the Spitfire comes to life and rolls forward to begin its journey to the fight, and moments later red-beard is high in the blue sky. Now they really are all up. There are no reserves left, held back just in case. The defence of the realm is now in the hands of a small number of men and their machines. The British pilots and their allies from countries all over the world are about to teach the Germans a lesson in what it is like to know defeat. It is their first real taste of defeat and a very small man in a bunker in Berlin is not amused. The tide has finally stopped running. A very, very small space in time has been created, a chance to draw breath, perhaps.

***

Once again he is very uncomfortable. He is aware the twitch has returned. He had given them a simple task. Why did they not carry out his orders as he gave them? When he gives an explicit instruction he expects it to be carried out. Which part of 'only bomb the airfields' do they not understand? What is so difficult about targeting the railways and docks and nothing else? We do not bomb civilians. We are Germans and I am Adolf Hitler. Somewhere deep inside he knows he should remain calm but he has lost his self-control. They have given the British the perfect excuse and they have accepted it with glee. They bombed his capitol city. A small raid only, but at least they had given him the ball back. The British had carried out this atrocity on purpose, but their bombing of homes by his Luftwaffe had been accidental. He holds the moral high ground and is surprised by the actions of the RAF. It is now his choice. He can do nothing or retaliate. He knows exactly what he is going to do; the German people will expect nothing less. He lets his emotions carry him into a full rage. He knows he should not make any decision when he is angry so he orders his pills. The man in the bunker takes his pills. They make him feel happy. He does not drink alcohol, but now he has passed the enraged stage of continually asking a fat man in a pristine white suit, "How many? We lost how many? How did this happen? You have betrayed me."

"They were waiting for us."

"Shit."

He goes to bed. He is not angry anymore, but he does not sleep. He sees planes falling from the sky. They are his planes. They are his boys and he is not prepared to lose any more at present. He sees his troops trying to fight through London and Birmingham and Manchester and Liverpool. He does not fancy fighting for Glasgow or Edinburgh. He knows that trying to subjugate Scotland will require massive numbers of troops. He knows that he will lose too many soldiers to take such a small country, which has no real significance of itself. There is another way to keep the British at bay. Britain is an island surrounded by a moat. It has too many ports that can be defended and supplied from the sea, from its Empire. They can defend every single little fishing hamlet, each one a fortress in the making. He knows that even the Irish might side with the British if they have too. He will not dare take Ireland. How could he subjugate the Welsh? No one has ever done that. Not even the Romans had dared to try for Scotland.

He has another plan and starts to dream about that instead. He makes up his mind; the invasion of England can wait. England and her neighbours have never waited - first mistake.

***

The little man in Berlin does not realise that many of his bombers have successfully reached their targets and have laid waste to vast areas of British towns and cities. On the ground the people have had enough. They want this to end. For many the end has already passed, but here on the ground there are many heroes. Small, insignificant people are holding their world together. They are not small in number as there are thousands of them watching for the falling devices, putting out fires that could burn for days. They, too, are fighting for their homes and lives, and those of their families and their friends. This is a civilian war. These people are not fighting for a cause. They care not about politicians and their causes. They are fighting for the woman next door whose son was killed at Dunkirk. They really do not care about the little man in Berlin. They wish he would just go away. They did not cause this. From out in the countryside and the highest of buildings they report on the advancing planes which carry their death loads. They fall and die as bombers deliver their premeditated, indiscriminate weapons, as masonry explodes beneath their feet. They join the unburied as night after night people hide in their shelters, in the crypts of churches, in the subterranean worlds of cellars and under-stair cupboards, of underground railways. The railways are the lifeblood of an island nation. Without them the nation cannot be fed, never mind defended.

A very small part of this nation is about to be defended by a small group of men who are at the end of their shift in a railway goods yard. They have already worked for forty-eight hours without sleep. The locomotives have been moved, since the air raid warning sounded, to the end of the sidings. They are mainly out in the countryside. It is easier to repair the wagons. Locomotives are in short supply. These men have worked through the air raid and are now being told to take to their shelters as they can do no more. Frank has stopped watching the high flyers and he has tried to find his father. He is looking skyward, now watching the glowing cinders dropping from the skies. The slate roofs of the nearby houses offer protection enough but they are building up on the embankment.

"Should we not be fire watching?" he asks the yard manager.

"No, lad. Not much we can do anyway. Tell you what, go and tell the shunting drivers to leave their locos in the yard and keep them stoked. Your legs are younger than mine. It is good to have you back, Frank. We need some younger men here; most of us are well past retirement. Bet your parents are pleased to see you." The manager smiles with his prior knowledge of what Frank had done. "Your father is over there, lad, and he could do with some help. He has been here since he returned early this morning."

Frank recognises the gaunt and tired figure of his father. Did he ever change his clothes? The stained boiler suit covering him head to foot looks like the same one he last saw him in.

"Long time no see, dad. I knew you would still be here, and on your own, of course."

"What are you doing here?"

"I work here."

"Since when?"

"Right now."

"Does your mother know you are home?" No words of welcome, just a small attempt at being human.

"Of course she knows. She is making us all a special tea, in spite of the mess."

"What mess?"

"Street got hit. No windows in the front of our house. I have boarded them up as best as I could."

"What for?"

"To keep out the cold."

"No, what's the special tea for?"

"Celebration."

"Nought to celebrate. We're about beat."

Silence followed their brief conversation.

"I've got my old job back. I've been demobbed."

More silence.

"Picked a good time to return, lad."

"Steam's dropping; your fire's too low; too much on top. No air flow."

"I have been driving trains for years, long since."

"Yes, but you never could raise a good fire."

Frank begins to rebuild the fire with small pieces of coal layered to the sides of the firebox. Slowly the heat rises and so does the pressure.

The last of the German Bombers has passed overhead. The final sticks of death have ceased to fall but the damage is already done. From the hilltop rising near the city they can see that its centre is clearly ablaze. A massive explosion on the docks shakes the very rock beneath their feet. A moment later fire and brimstone rain down on the carefully arranged shunting yards. They have witnessed the total destruction of a munitions' ship. Shards of metal begin clanging on the roof of their cab. Frank nods to his father.

"Look."

A locomotive begins to pull away very slowly in the yard, heading towards the track to the centre of the city. A small fire in the first wagon is gaining hold in the breeze coming up-track from the burning city.

"He needs to go the other way before it spreads."

"I'll go," says Frank.

He takes the emergency lantern with him. His father watches as he sprints across the debris-covered shunting yard towards the train and the nearby houses.

The burning train stops. Frank jumps on to the plate.

"Reverse the engines."

The stoker is dead, pinned into place by a metal sheet which has cut through his shoulder and the controls. The train driver is trying to free the controls.

"It's stuck, lad. Only goes forward. I was trying to pull it clear of the housing."

"It's spreading the fire."

"Is he dead?"

Frank nods. "What's the load?"

"Munitions."

Other men are already uncoupling the engine and tender. Frank can see his old friend Peter climbing back into the destroyed signal box, the levers still pointing in their self-determined angles. He waves to Frank and points beyond the train. His father is slowly shunting the engine in reverse towards the wagons. Frank jumps out and runs towards his father, knowing he will see the red light still glimmering in the firelight. In the space of moments the second engine is in place. Now it is time for skilled hands as Frank again stokes the firebox, carefully bringing up the heat again and regaining full pressure. His father is taking up the slack and wagons begin to clink away from each other, leaving behind the burning wagon.

"George has got them well-organised," says Frank senior. "But who the hell is that in his pyjamas?" They both laugh as they recognise John Gee, who is organising the uncoupling of the still-smouldering wagons. Slowly they are being spread out along the tracks towards the countryside. Pete, the signalman, is boxing clever tonight. He even gets one of the wagons under a water tower where it is literally cooled down by the water that would normally go into the loco. He has just staggered the last of wagons when the first wagon disappears in an explosion which shatters the windows of the nearby houses. But they remain standing.

As the final debris from the explosions rain down the railwaymen are literally thrown to the ground, where they scramble for cover under the giant metal monsters that are now offering their protective shells. Tomorrow their operators can fire them up again and make these heavy machines do what they are meant to do. The quiet hissing noise of the decompressing steam reassures the sheltering men, making them feel secure as it is a noise they own, one they have created themselves every day since they were lads themselves. And like the final glowing embers of their own lives, the warming fires in the chambers guide them to sleep.

\*\*\*

Forgive me if I appear to repeat myself but I lost many sons from this village in the first Great War. I try to recall them as often as possible but I think my memory is failing. They said it was the war to end all wars. Millions died; sometimes the sun rose and set and another million men or more had died. How was it possible? But this war, too, came and went, replaced by the whisperings of fanatics who had not yet given up hope. They still believed the first war continued and it did not take them too long to start again. The people of my village are sad. Once again their sons, brothers and fathers go off to defend their way of life against evil, and again some of them do not return, but this is a different kind of conflict as it is over in days. The crops have barely had chance to put on any growth when the radios begin to tell the people what they should do once the Germans arrive. There is nothing to fear. These people claim to be liberators. But my villagers already feel liberated. They will not know what to do with any more freedom. But then their radios are taken away and they realise what this new form of liberty will mean. And still they do not really notice any change. They know of a great, devastating defeat of their army in the North, near the Belgian border, and that their allies have gone. They, too, were defeated, but lived on to fight again another day. But the lives of my people remain the same. They carry on working their farms, making their wines and growing their food. Some things are difficult to obtain but if you know the right people you can still get them. Some human beings appear to grow in adversity.

They keep their secret radios hidden and it is sometimes difficult to find out what is going on but they know the war has changed from the land to the air and the sea; and cities are being raised to the ground. Their liberators have failed to pursue the British across the Channel and so have decided to fight someone else instead. My villagers try to go about their lives in exactly the same way as before. People begin to arrive from other parts of the country but they are quickly assimilated into the population. Their accent is different but they speak the same language. Some of the liberators are nearby but they do not try to stay in this village. They would not have been made welcome. The people of my village have long memories and great patience. They are more than capable of waiting for a foreign foe to make up its mind to go back to where they came from.

# PART TWO

"We are to sweep south. Intelligence is saying that the French are re-organising. They may yet defend Paris." For once it is Heinz who is shaking his friend awake.

"Where are we going?" Adi asks Heinz, who is barely awake himself.

"Destination Bordeaux, or further; how about a weekend in Biarritz, perhaps cross the border into Spain? Just to have a look, of course."

"Of course - as long as there are girls on the beaches."

"The further south we get the more the French will think they are occupied. They won't like it if we occupy their Atlantic ports. Then you can have your pick of the girls. Not that any of them will have you."

"The French Fleet is heading towards the Med."

"Where it can do nothing."

"How far are we from Bordeaux?"

"More like how long- three days I would say."

"This does not feel possible. In three days we will have occupied the west coast of France."

"*Oui, mon Capitaine, nous avons arrivé. Ou sont les femmes?*"

Heinz hits Adi, causing him to lose his newly-lit cigarette. It disappears through a hole in the floor next to the clutch plate.

"Wonderful," says Heinz. "Your son died bravely at the end of a cigarette butt carelessly disposed of by his gunner."

"Do not worry, *Capitaine*, there is nothing underneath."

"Like your skull."

Soon they will be all that is left of a substantial force of men who have been gradually whittled down to less than two hundred to occupy a major French Port, their numbers gradually growing less each time as they leave behind enough troops to occupy a town or village. They will not have long to wait for the actual ceasefire.

On their final night just outside Bordeaux they leave their transports to walk about, smoke and reflect on the fact that they are still alive, but for how long. They all have the same unnerving thought, that this is just too easy. Yet the following day proves to be just the same and soon they will return home as heroes.

As his friend Adi says, "Time for the girls."

But here there are no girls, no reception committee, just shuttered windows and barred doors. There is no one in sight, not even a mad dog, as his grandfather would have said.

"Orders are to go directly to the port. Some of the French Army has tried to land in Brittany. They may come here too."

"Two hundred rifles against how many?"

"There's talk of at least a hundred thousand Frenchies getting away with the British."

"Prepare to die."

"If they come we retreat. Be ready to leave soon." A simple order given to soldiers taking their first beer at a bar still open on the docks. Payment in cigarettes and chocolate is perfectly acceptable to someone who can manage a bar in such a place. Armies do not march on beer; they will have to stop too often. But they know how to barter and for some reason men all over the world seem to prefer beer as their drink of celebration. Adi is astonished when his friend takes the beer he offers.

"Adi, does it ever get any better than this?" Heinz looks at his bottle as if expecting it to answer him.

"*Nein, mein fuhrer.*" They both wonder what the real Fuhrer would think of his joke.

"Indeed, *mon ami.*" Heinz decides not to take any further risks as they drink their beer.

They sit and wait for the fight that never comes. They remove their boots, socks and tunics, roll up their trousers and paddle in the warm shallows while other, braver souls splashed naked in the cold Atlantic waves roaring onto the shore.

The next day they are dispatched to Marseilles. Someone is trying to sink the French Fleet. They are given all the easy jobs; a brief respite that is not to last.

***

The young men are coming and going at a faster rate than he dare think about. The losses are beyond comprehension. Heinz counts the battles since France; he leaves out Greece and Yugoslavia as they did not lose many in terms of dead. Now he thinks of Smolensk and the other places. He realises that they have lost millions of wounded or dead. He looks at the men around him and can only count ten that he knows well. The others are more like boys, perhaps four or five years younger than his age. When he shaves in the morning he sees an old face in the mirror. He wants to ask those left behind in Germany how it feels to wash and shave with warm, soapy water. He melts snow in his metal mug over a candle and looks to see if any food has arrived. He sees young, healthy men arrive in October, full of energy and bravado; by November they are dying. The cold, lack of food and simple illnesses take their toll. The Russians have not fired a shot at them for weeks. It is too cold. The enemy waits in their winter. They are used to waiting during their winter. They need do nothing. Their supplies are coming from the East. Nothing comes from the West. The promises of the fat man in the white suit in Berlin never materialise. Why should he worry? He is in his warm, safe flat in Berlin. There are no fat men on the front line in Russia, only hungry, demoralised, poorly equipped soldiers who will fight with what little they have.

Standing outside the dugout he feels the cracking wind strip away the heat from his body in seconds. The November day is clear and he can see the domes of the churches of Moscow. They are this close; he measures their heights with the space between forefinger and thumb and places them as a photograph in his memory. He has drawn the spidery outline of the buildings he can see in his small black book, making special notes he will send to Hannah. He had so looked forward to visiting the sites of Moscow. He had believed the local people would welcome their arrival. The war would be over for them and they would have been set free and Communism would have been defeated. The other cities had not failed in what they had offered. He had enjoyed Paris and Belgrade. He now accepts that he would never set foot in Moscow. They know the Russians are preparing a counter-offensive. It is just a matter of time until the snow stops falling.

***

Hannah's father smiles at the daily arrival of his letters. They may be days old but they are regular. He usually meets the postman and they exchange a few words about their war wounds as they had served together on the Western Front in the Great War. The postman usually holds up Heinz's letters with some remark such as, 'Must be love,' 'More letters from the East,' 'This one has still got snow on.' They laugh together as the address on the envelope always says, 'Miss U Hannah', followed by the address. The postman is allowed to be in on the knowledge.

"Do you think she realises what it means, Joseph?" He still finds it strange to call his former sergeant by his first name.

"I don't know. I will call her and ask her."

"No."

"Hannah?" Too late.

Hannah appears at the front door.

"Thomas would like to ask you a question."

"Yes Thomas?"

"I have another letter for you from your young man in Russia. He must think about you all the time. You must feel very special for him to write so often." Thomas glowers at Joseph.

"How often did you write to your wives when you were in love and away from your homes?"

"Every day," they chime together, like a well-rehearsed line from a long-running play.

"I rest my case," she answers as she notes the special 'U' before her name.

"Unusual how he writes your name." Now it is Thomas' turn to receive the glare from his old friend.

"I hadn't noticed," she replies, and retreats to the darkness of the old house to open her letter, unable to wait for the contents to reveal themselves. His letters are sometimes quite short but still overwhelming in their detail. Sometimes they just say he is warm and well-fed, no more than a soldier could ask. He always ends his letters with a salutation to the Fuhrer as he knows the censors are lazy and will pass it more easily with such a statement. His letters are always positive but carry an underlying theme of information to describe what is really happening. Often his poetry contains simple descriptions to enable her to know what he is doing, or where he is. She opens the sealed jacket with a large kitchen knife.

She reads carefully, trying to imagine where he is, knowing that his words are some kind of code:

*For Hannah. Number #53*

*Snow–capped buildings, domed in gold, are within their grasp,*

*And like mortals making old; on unclear days, are afraid to ask;*

*For a city belonging to others, under the siege for life,*

*She is defended by brothers; out-waiting the strife,*

*That may come in the morning, as battle is engaged,*

*And without warning; her defenders are enraged,*

*By our very presence; as we seem to be victorious.*

*But in our defence, it had appeared glorious.*

*Time has now sacked, and withdrawn its jury;*

*And we are attacked by the winter's cold fury.*

*Fingers stick to gun metal, which causes forces*

*Of ice-bonds elemental between skin and sources,*

*Candle-warmed oil is sprayed, releasing the tension,*

*Pain is delayed; we wait with apprehension.*

*(We start again tomorrow, ready for anything,*

*Excepting the sorrow, and the sadness of living.)*

At the end of his other words he writes of his love for her and their unborn child.

Hannah holds the papers to her lips. "Stay safe," she whispers to herself as their child moves within her emotions.

\*\*\*

The counter offensive is vicious when it comes. The soldiers in white are not the Russians they are used to. They look Asian. They seem to welcome the snow and cold. They are specialist soldiers who know how to fight in these conditions. They are well-equipped, with a clear sense of purpose. Very soon they are in full retreat from the outskirts of Moscow and know that to leave their own wounded behind is pointless. Men ask to be shot rather than become prisoners. Heinz senses a new trend and does not like the direction it is pointing. He receives his wish to go home to

Hannah and their soon-to-be-born child. His regiment has suffered heavy losses at the forefront of the attack on Russia and so is the first to be withdrawn and sent home - fortunately for them. Now they will receive proper care for their injuries.

***

She sees him first. He is barely recognisable as the healthy young husband she proudly packed off to war. He can barely walk, and is being supported by two orderlies. Her father stands next to her. He squeezes her hand as he shakes his head. Tears fill her eyes as she watches him move slowly towards them, and a small, completely-formed child within her moves in reaction. He has been looking forward to forthcoming fatherhood. Hannah thought the baby would make a wonderful Christmas present for them both. She can offer little else, except her love.

A guard blocks her path. "That's my husband." The soldier still does not move.

"Young man," Hannah's father says, putting his arm across the man's chest. "We would like to collect our son." He turns to show him the Iron Cross that he is proudly wearing around his neck. The soldier comes to attention and moves to one side. Heinz just stands looking at them.

And like millions of women who wait for their men to come home from war, she reaches out to him. She places her hand in his and waits for the pressure that will tell her that all would be well. And like millions of men who come home from wherever they have gone he is confused and ill at ease. He lets her take him home. She knows it will be a long time before the pressure comes that will tell her that all is well. Sophie is born three days later.

It is not long after that he is again called to duty in spite of his wounds. Experienced soldiers are difficult to find.

***

"Back again?" She is standing at her bedroom door, almost smiling at her Polish Pilot Officer. "Do you know how difficult it was to get you to England? How come you are back here again?"

"It's a long story. I lost another one of their planes."

"Shot down once is bad luck but twice is poor flying."

"Took quite a few with me this time. Better plane, the Spitfire. Remarkable machine. Do you know you can get within a hundred metres of a German fighter and still they miss you?"

"Not always in your case."

61

"I won't be trying again."

"What do you mean?"

"I am not going back to England. I missed half of the war travelling through France and Spain. Anyway I'd rather be dead than face the Bay of Biscay again, even in a submarine. Portsmouth is a long way from Gibraltar and the Spaniards are fascists too. They don't even know there is a war on. The fun is over in England for the moment. The RAF and some of our lads gave those German flyer boys a lesson they will not be forgetting too soon. I missed most of it. I arrived too late. Then they would not give me a plane. They said I had lost one of theirs already in France. I thought it was only the Germans who kept an account of such things."

"So that's three planes you lost, not two. You could lose the air war on your own without even trying."

"Not really. I ditched the first one in Belgium after Poland had been invaded. That was one of our planes. We were ordered to get out to France. Most of the others got there before me. I stayed on as long as possible."

"And the second one?"

"Don't remember too much. There were just too many of them and not enough of us. Bailed out just in time near Lille. I could just see the outline of England. I never saw the plane crash. Could still be up there you know. She was a game old bird - a Hurricane. Do you know they are made from wood? Brilliant. You just need a tree, a saw, and a hammer and some nails."

"And the last one?"

"I needed to get back here. I left it burning on some German ship in the Channel. Just off the coast. I thought, if I have to swim, so will they. They had been firing at me all day. Shame about the plane, but at least I ended up back in France."

"And in my bed."

"Sorry about that. It is a very nice bed. Very warm and comfortable. Space enough for two. It would be nice to have someone to share it with."

"Exactly what I was thinking." She smiles to herself.

He pulls the covers back. She places a pile of clothes on the pillow.

"For me?"

"No, my brother's room is too small for two so he will share in here with you."

"And I came all this way to see you."

"As you can see, here I am."

"And you would be preferable to your brother."

"Not a chance."

He is about to speak again as he rubs the stubble of his days-old beard.

"Are you drooling again?" She throws the clean sheets at him. "You can make your own bed now."

\*\*\*

The landscape of Kursk shapes the movement of his field glasses to its contours. It has not yet healed from earlier battles and has an unnatural look with few trees; the only real cover is the slope of the land itself. Heinz makes a mental note that to his right is a small wood just beyond the edge of the open field. He realises something is missing from the hot, dry landscape: animals and birds. And this is farmland but there are no crops, just the unpicked leftovers from the last time these fields were worked. The only animals here are the ones who carry weapons of destruction. He knows they are there waiting for them to make the first move. He has given specific instructions that no one is to go forward until his tank moves. Tank battles are often more like a game of chess until the killing starts. Everyone on both sides knows of bluff and counter-bluff. Put one of your tanks in an open position and then show it retreating; follow at your peril. The gap opens, pour through or take the kill and find you are cut off on slightly lower ground than you anticipated. The chess game has started.

The days of blitzkrieg chess are over. Air supremacy is now all that matters. Russian planes are of poorer quality but at least they have them. Their tanks are not much better but they are also many and now they have better trained and faster moving troops, who fight without fear.

Heinz sees the Russian Tank and fires, but the barrel of the enemy tank quickly slips from view.

"Wait." He speaks to no one in particular. One of his tanks begins to move forward, followed by the others. He breaks radio silence. "I said to wait for me." Too late already and he knows it. He is the only tank holding position.

"Forward slowly." He needs the view from the top of the rise. He watches as the other German tanks reach the objective prematurely, and start to explode one by one as their weaker under-armour gives way to penetrating shells. Nothing is left when this happens - no bodies to retrieve, no remains of sons to be sent home for burial, unless you want to send flesh minced by metal splinters. Fire, they tell you, is the worst fear. Not so. Millions of shards of metal cutting you to pieces can be far worse. No one ever really knows as death is usually the only outcome.

He reaches the rim but the outcome of this engagement is already decided. Two more tanks disappear when their turrets are ripped off.

"Shell in the breech, do not fire. Repeat, do not fire. Full reverse." An order given for survival. They have taken two hits. Their howitzer 88 mm cannon has taken shrapnel after a shell deflects off a track. They are going nowhere and there is no way they can survive these odds. They cannot now even return fire.

"Out, now. That means everybody and now means now." His driver gives them extra seconds by hitting a wall, allowing the front of the tank to be buried by protective masonry which traps him in the small compartment. He has paid the ultimate price.

"Down." They fall into the soft earth at the edge of the field as numerous Russian tanks started to use the disabled tank for target practice. Others are now running across the battlefield in an effort to escape from their burning vehicles, which pop with the same sound as you get when you drop a bottle of fizzy lemonade. They are caught in the scything machine gun fire.

"Go right." The wall offers protection and a stray round has punched a fortunate opening in the wall.

"Roll to the hole and through. Don't wait for anyone. Prepare for infantry."

None comes. The Russian tanks continue to use the wall as fire practice and are slowly cutting off their line of retreat. The Russian infantrymen are still sheltering behind their tanks. Why take the risk? The Germans crawl and roll into what is left of the small wood; splintered stumps provide at least some cover.

"Through the woods and wait together at the other side." Vegetation always grows thicker on the south side of a house, wall or forest. As they run through the partly destroyed wood it becomes denser and covers their visual retreat in thick summer leaves. 'At least they have to guess where we are now,' Heinz thinks. Their rapid movements are brought to a halt by a small drainage stream at the edge of the wood. Its sloping banks provide further cover.

'Just like the trenches,' he thinks as he slides downwards to take cover for what is about to become a First World War battle.

"Pass the word to follow me and do what I do. I can get you out of this if you do what I say." He has no idea what he intends to do, but he watches carefully as the smoke from the burning tanks begins to follow the breeze. The smoke thickens as the flames are fanned by the wind and the smell of burning rubber joins the conflagration. The hot diesel in the fuel tanks reaches its ignition temperature and begins to burn ferociously; and now the atmosphere has changed. The Russians are no longer looking for them. The Russians are at least having the same problems with the burning debris of the battlefield but they can at least go forward out of the drifting smoke.

"Wet your clothes if you can. Cover your eyes and mouths with a damp cloth." Men in vests and shorts are suddenly half naked as they seek refuge from the dense smoke. The twenty men pour water from cupped hands over each other's heads as they use their vests as crude gas masks. Heinz knows it will give them five minutes extra at most.

Heinz and the Russian tank commander catch sight of each other in their own field glasses. The Russian is caught in the thick swirling fog and he looks like he is breathing with difficulty. The Russian tank turns forward and away from the line of smoke and past the exploding vehicles at the rear of the German tanks.

The infantry do what all good infantrymen always do: they survive and take land. They go forward with the protection of huge lumps of steel. They, too, are covering their faces, but they have their gas masks, which they are holding onto their faces - limited protection but at least something. Heinz continues to watch the lead tank as they go past the battle lines and into the next field. He can now see other German soldiers on the exposed flank, one of whom is looking at him through binoculars. He signals him to stay down and a moment later to move towards the rear of the Russians. In a small field in the middle of a prairie a small company of German soldiers assembles to the rear of the Russian Army. On either side of the field men have died in their hundreds. Within minutes they are all that is left of a huge spearhead of German tanks. Now they wait for dark and the fires to cease burning.

They know they will not be rescued and the Russian second wave will mop up any survivors. The other surviving tank commanders agree that they should leave in groups of five and head south west. Heinz decides he will be last to leave.

***

The Russian advance stopped during the night - for what reason is anyone's guess. Their infantry has now caught up fully in numbers and are reinforcing the front line. Many tank commanders would have preferred to fight without infantry support. They do not see how they are helped by walking men. Often they wait for hours for the reserve troops to catch up to the front line anyway. Heinz watches as some pockets of trapped German infantry break cover and a single Russian tank simply destroys them; another scene from another war. He turns to look at who is left. They are mostly men that he knows.

"We are staying here and holding our ground. Spread out and play dead."

"We are dead." Common words that pass through similar minds.

"Stay down and when I give the order we are going back towards our rendezvous point and then East, but we are going to do it quietly and crawl if we have to." Men start making peace with their gods, their wives and children.

"What are we waiting for, *Capitaine, mon ami*?" Adi made it, too.

"I thought you were dead." Heinz grimaces at his inappropriate choice of words.

"Not to worry; I soon will be."

"I am waiting for the mosquitoes."

"What, British planes?"

"No the biting kind."

"Why?"

"Watch and see."

The intense heat of the day remains the same. No one now moves except the Russian soldiers who begin to climb into wagons, preoccupied with the tasks of nightfall and whining insects instead of bullets. They have won the battle. They are expecting a peaceful evening. What is left of what would have been a perfectly normal summer's day in peacetime is nearly complete. The sun is now to their advantage as anyone looking for them will be looking directly into the setting sun.

"Now," he says. "It is time to go, and no slapping at the insects. Take your bites like men."

He waits until he is last man left and starts to run in the same direction as the others. He is stopped suddenly, aware of the tearing sensation of metal on skin. He has run in to a simple farmer's fence in the undergrowth at the edge of the field. He is trapped and cannot move for fear of screaming in pain.

"I am coming back to get you. Keep still, *mon Capitaine*."

Staying still is not a problem. On the wire he passes out; starvation and tiredness have taken their toll, and his body has decided that it has had enough of the searing pain. Death would be better than this. He thinks briefly of his wife and child and the choice is made for him.

It is all he can do not to scream. He did not expect to see the dawn. The Russians are so close he could touch them with a long pole. He has run into very old, peasant-made barbed wired. For a moment he thinks of the soldiers of the First War. In the dark he remembered his high school chemistry and focuses on this, as rust mingles with his blood. Iron is in the blood, but this has ripped through his tunic and torn the flesh. He has had other injuries but none that hurt like this. He is ripped. In silence, he slowly tries to disentangle himself from his crown of barbs. They grip tighter. He feels wet in various parts of his lower body. It is not sweat and it is not blood. Urine has run down his groin and legs. He blinks his eyes rapidly, trying to clear his vision as his brow produces more blood than he realised he had. He knows this is not a good sign, but his mind is running on. He remains very still in the thorn-sharp hedge of the very open field. He knows he will die soon as in the early light Russian troops pass within a range so close that he can see the stubble on one man's face. There is no doubt that he has been seen.

The man looks filthy, but his uniform is in good condition and how Heinz envies the thick-soled boots. He waits to be shot and hopes it will be a clean kill. But he stills his eyes completely and uses a trick he learnt as a little boy with plenty of bullies around. His father told him to just stare them out and wait for them make the first move. Then go for the groin. However you fared, this would ensure respect afterwards. Forget about fair play and punching below the waist; if you land the first kick and it is in the balls he will never fight you again. If you fail he will still be wary of you. "Stay still and wait," he commands himself.

His own blood stings his eyes but they remain glazed and now focussed on a distant, burnt-out tank. He is covered in blood and can feel it running down his neck. He watches the enemy soldier ignore him, a large rump disappears over the edge of the ditch and moments later reappears on the other side. He disappears again completely into the scrub and the front line has passed him by in a matter of seconds. He is obviously not worth a bullet, and has been left for dead even if he has been seen. No wonder they are losing the war. They are outnumbered by four to one and although they have the better equipment they have no firepower because they have little left to fire with. Excellent rifles but by the time you have killed four of them with yours the fifth one gets you with the butt of his empty rifle and then takes yours and uses it to provide the final finish. The Russian soldiers have the greatest motivation of all soldiers. If the enemy does not kill you, your commanders will shoot you if they suspect you of cowardice.

He waits until can hear nothing, and is still until even the sound of battle has moved away. The hedge rustles and another very dirty, oil-stained face appeared. This one is smiling.

"Idiot," Heinz whispers.

"Maybe, but I told you I would return." He shows the wire cutters to his tank commander. They have been an effective team.

"Where have you been?"

"Avoiding their patrols. They've got men to spare; and I mean to spare."

"You need a shave, soldier, and your uniform is filthy. Defaulters parade tomorrow at six a.m."

"Sir."

Adi snips quietly at the barbed wire, freeing his commander and friend, but he is unable to clear the whole entangled mess without attracting attention. He looks at the man he has known for four years and is unable to discuss with him the fact that it is over for Germany. Perhaps Heinz already knows it is, but Adi is unwilling to discuss it with an officer, even if he is a friend. You can be shot for voicing even the simplest of statements. Something in common with their enemy, but the motivation is entirely different. In the last three days they have retreated as far as a man can run in that time. Back through the same villages they pillaged on the way to Moscow. Now they are burning them. The peasants are long gone. They know where to hide and how to protect their families. The sexual bravado on the way forward is missing from the retreat. They have no time to eat, never mind think about a girl or two.

Part of his skin stays behind with the barbs. He is about to scream and remembers the tactic of hissing through your teeth. It sounds like a bullet in flight as it passes his ears. He can feel what is left of his teeth grinding as pain travels from one place to another. The wire is now not cutting him, just his uniform.

"We should go now and finish the rest later."

Heinz nods in agreement. He is now free to move.

"South East, we have better defences to the South East."

They move away quietly, leaving behind their decimated army. He looks and sees a relatively small field and estimates one hundred dead, mainly German, and this is just one small field across a front of so many. So much for stand and defend screamed at them from the little man in Berlin; so much for the Russians being subhuman and easy to beat. 'They will not fight you. They hate their government. They just want to sit around smoking and drinking vodka, and if capable, have sex with their women, or yours, or each other.' They fought as though they had the greatest country on earth. Nothing is as it should have been. The greatest fighting machine in history is being destroyed by a lower species of human beings. Clearly they are not all of that calibre.

Are they the only survivors? The noise of battle has stopped except for single gun shots. They both know what that means. The troops at the rear are now cleansing the field of battle and removing anything of value from the dead or those about to die. They sometimes spare officers, but not SS. They will die if caught. They are well known in these parts. The burning of villages mark the SS out as most wanted. Both men discard anything that is not of use and begin to walk towards the South East. In his head he knows they have one chance to survive, and if this means moving in parallel to the Russian front they can just find an opportunity. They will also need an excellent story as to why they were not killed. He is working on that already and has begun to plan a small but sophisticated piece of intelligence about the whereabouts of the Russian reserves. It will purchase a number of things: their lives, food, and a right to some sort of transfer or leave and a fresh start. They agree on their story and start to collect documents from dead officers. It will tell High Command the sort of thing they think they want to know. Who is fighting where? It will not make any difference but someone in logistics will be promoted. He has no idea what it is about to do to him.

\*\*\*

Two weeks later Adolf Hitler emerges from his bunker and pins another Iron Cross onto Heinz's brand new uniform. You would really not know there was a war going on very close by. He notices the Fuhrer's hands are shaking. Their eyes never meet, but here is the man they once looked up to. Now, he has brought nothing but destruction to nearly every country in Europe and beyond.

The dead eyes of the Fuhrer make their own statement. "Soldier; go home to your family and friends." One front line soldier speaks to another.

"And can I come with you? This is over but no one dares tell me." One who knows the end is near and can do nothing about it.

Heinz forgets to salute at the end of the award of his medal but no one seems to care or take notice. Young, excited boys are also receiving awards. They are excited beyond belief and will be dead very soon. They remember the formalities. Their hero pats each one gently on the cheek like a nice old man would do to his grown grandson as a fond farewell on his death bed. An apology?

Heinz returns to find his regiment has been pulled off the line and sent to France again. The battle for Kursk has been well and truly lost. It is time to go home, again.

"I baptise thee," he says, choking back his tears. "In the Name of the Father and the Son and the Holy Ghost."

"He needs a name," says the midwife. "Or he cannot enter heaven."

"Such nonsense." His reply is somewhat muffled. "He is a child."

Hannah is weeping. "I need to hold my baby."

"Not a good idea," says the midwife. "We do not normally allow even this."

"You don't allow? Who are you not to allow? This is our son. Our beloved son. We will do as we see fit." His son.

He places the still-born child in his wife's arms and then holds them both closely.

"Leave us." A soldier's command. The midwife needs no further persuasion. "Look at his hair. He is very dark - like you."

"My grandfather's name was David."

"So we have chosen."

He looks at the perfectly formed child with the slight blue tinge, indicating a lack of oxygen before birth.

Two days later they wrap their son in a linen cloth and place him into the simple box made by Hannah's father. He is buried in the same grave as her grandfather.

"Look after his little soul, granddad, and keep him safe. Wait for me. I won't be long." The card is signed, *mama*.

"We will think of him often," he says to Hannah.

He has chosen a brief passage to read. "'Before I formed you in the womb I knew you, before you were born I set you apart; I appointed you as a prophet to the nations.'"

"You will always be part of us," he whispers as the soil level reaches the surface, covering the small box set to one side of the main grave, leaving a small, rectangular space in the earth.

"What do you feel?" she asks of him.

"Grief," Heinz says to Hannah. "Is what I feel. It is what you are left with when you have nowhere to place your love; a ghost or an echo of something that was once beautiful, alive and vital. That is why when you feel the loss of love that you feel grief. But this can be overcome, unlike death, which is permanent. Do I believe in ghosts? Absolutely. The ultimate ghost is your love for someone who has died. Such grief wanders forever. It has no home. This is what we mean when we say we are haunted by a spirit. Do they still love us? Ask them and they will tell you. The answer is yes, yes, yes. That is what I feel."

"Did my baby love me? Did he love us?"

His words are good for her, but they sound academic; a distant discussion about a phrase in a book that perhaps he had discovered.

"I think our child knew before he was born that he was loved and cared for. I really believe that. Even by me. Would he not have known our voices, especially yours, Hannah?"

"Do you love me?" A deliberate question seeking his reassurances.

"Of course I love you."

"How do you love me?"

"Like this."

He places his hand to her face as if to kiss her. She covers his mouth with her hand so he holds her wrist as if to move her hand away.

"Promise me you will never betray me and Sophie."

"I have given you my oath." Heinz needs to close his eyes and sleep. He stops thinking when he is asleep.

"Say it," she demands. "I want to hear you say it."

"I will never betray you, or our daughter." He moves his hand away and touches her face. "I love you both too much to do such a thing."

"Do you not expect the same of me?"

"I have no need. I know you will not."

"Ask me."

"No."

"Scared of the answer?"

He thinks she is mocking him. "No I just know. It is not within you."

"Sometimes men and women commit acts of betrayal for a greater good."

"You read too many books Hannah. Anyhow that is not a betrayal."

"Explain that to me." She has the sound in her voice that lets him know he cannot win and he tries to reduce the situation to normal. How can they be talking like this when they have just buried their son?

"It is different for a man and a woman."

"How so?" A terse reply; wanting a fight.

"A woman may take another man because he can provide her with food and shelter. She is the one who is taken. Men do the taking. But if it meant it would save your child's life then you would do it."

"How would you feel if that happened to me while you are away?"

"Are you trying to tell me something?"

"No." But for the first time since he met Hannah he is uneasy; a dangerous feeling for a man about to go away again. He moves his head away and rests it on the pillow. She rolls away from him and lies with her back to him.

"For what it is worth Hannah, I do love you and in case you do not know, I loved our child. I have seen death come in many ways but this death is the most devastating of all. I wish it had been me."

For the first time ever as they are about to sleep her head is not resting in its normal place on his shoulder. If it had been he would have felt the tears she is weeping for a small, lost soul and the way her husband appears to be so distant from her, his emotions restrained, everything is flat, methodical, unreal, his soul apparently disconnected; his soul, too, is lost.

***

"We could walk by the river if you would like. The baby is ready." He notices how Sophie looks relatively well-nourished, her clothes clean and tidy. Hannah looks tired; her clothes are old and worn out. They will not last. He is appalled to see her wearing one of his old raincoats.

"I am not going out with you dressed like that. You look like a tramp in that coat."

She begins to cry. "I do not have a coat. I have enough to feed our child; there is nothing left from the money you send. My father tries to help but his pension is small and of little value."

"What happens to the money I send?"

"Everything is expensive; there is little in the shops. We have to barter for everything."

He notices that she is no longer wearing her wedding rings. He does not comment, but a question has been locked into his brain. This is a question he can never ask, so there cannot be a response. Just what is she bartering?

He leaves the house, trying to avoid further confrontation and follows his father-in-law to the park, taking Sophie out of the unpleasant atmosphere that he knows he set between them.

\*\*\*

She finds his letter the day after he leaves. They have barely spoken a civilised word. They had so looked forward to this short time together, but he has turned his back on her. He can hear her crying softly; he does not know how to reach out to her. He is in a room that is not his, in a house that is not of his making, with a wife and daughter that are strangers. The open window allows the soundless night to be the echo of the silence that has entered their lives. They are no longer in charge of their own destiny.

She feels the warmth of his body leave the bed. He moves quietly to the baby's crib. He pauses. Hannah knows he is leaving. Silently she asks for the man who she married to come back to her. The front door of the house clicks shut and he is gone; she is alone.

\*\*\*

Her father breaks the silence. "He's gone, then?"

She nods dumbly, tears on the edge of dark-rimmed eyes. "He never even said goodbye. He kissed the baby and left. I watched him from the window. He never looked back. I heard him go."

"This is not about you." Her father notes the unopened envelope on the table. "And it is not about him either."

"Then what is it about?"

"War changes people." His own wife had not known what to do with him when he returned from his war. For months he did not leave the house. He worked in his garden. In the end it was Hannah's arrival that brought him to his senses.

"He will return, you know."

"No father, he expects to die."

"Did he tell you this?"

"No. It is what I feel. He has reached the end. I think he wants to die. He can do no more. Something bad has happened to him; something very bad and the death of our baby is the final straw. It is his pride which is keeping him going. Look at what he left next to the baby's cot."

Her father takes the medal from her and holds it in the flat of his hand. He knows what this means to a soldier. The dark cloak is descending. The empty eyes of his men in the trenches had said it all. They had already said goodbye to their loved ones. They had gone away anyway. Many would never recover even if they had survived the physical carnage and death. Mental injury is so much worse than physical. It is intangible, immeasurable, and invisible to all except the victim.

"It is a pressure that builds and won't go away," he tells her. "It is about serving a master that you no longer believe in. You become fixed by the moment and you cannot remove it from your mind. It goes around and around. You cannot break the cycle in your mind; it has taken over itself. You are no longer in charge. In my war they called it shell shock or trench fever. You know it has taken over when you start to think, 'I will die, no I won't. I might. So what? Death is preferable than this.' Then if you survive the next engagement you are ecstatic for a short period, but that does not last long. You want to be with your mates whose bodies are still on the battle field. Guilt creeps in like a thief in the night. You would have welcomed death at that moment because it would at least be over."

"Hannah, read his letter. Men are often better on paper than when speaking of their love. He does love you, you know."

"Does he? How do you know?"

"He told me, and no I am not just saying it to make you feel better. Read his letter."

"Later."

"He will return. I will go and get him myself. He is not on active duty anymore."

She smiles weakly at her father. "They are all on active duty now. I think he just wants to die. It is the only way he can escape."

***

In the window of his room Heinz views the ancient mirror of the river and sees a body which he knows is his own but he does not recognise it. The legs still carry the scars of the cutting trajectories of heavy-calibre machine gun fire. His back looks like it has been scourged with an ancient whip, and a crown of thorns, hidden by his hair, has been added for good measure. Forty lashes and more have scarred him forever. As with many men he had liked his body. In his maturity he could not believe his good fortune. The hair and eyes are the right colour - blue eyes, blond hair make him the perfect specimen. His physique honed by army training and swimming, had stood the test of time. It was not pride he felt but simply that in the beginning he had felt good.

In the glass of the silvered mirror, he traces the ruptures of his skin, scars caused by his basic instinct to survive and escape. The marks are still on a living body, thanks to his friend. His mad, lovable friend who now has no family but the crew of a tank and who has taken him from the moment of death to survival; not all people called Adolf are evil. His Adolf should have received the medal. Not for his bravery or beliefs, or because his nickname is Adi, but because he is his friend and does not only fight for his cause but would have the courage to tell him when he is wrong. If he was going to raise an issue he would cough into a clean white handkerchief, as if trying to hide what he will be about to say. Those handkerchiefs, he must have thousands of them, and they are always clean. He never did ask Adi how he manages to keep them so clean.

The sharpness of the land reveals itself to his narrowed eyes. The light is sharp too and the land shimmers from the heat of the day. The ancient glass disturbs the image, blurring the focus, forcing his eyes to flick and seek a clear view that will not come. This glass is made for comfort, not for viewing. It is not made to watch the world through; such glass came later than this. Light bends when it enters a new medium, it does not move of itself but it is forced to change direction and again as it leaves by an altered but parallel path. Old bands of a dark grey metal keep the glass in its rightful place. Its leaden squares force an image of distance, each a frame of a particular, distorted photograph. The heat of the day has climbed to its maximum. Sensible creatures have made their way into the shade; humans, too, have withdrawn from the burning ball of fire. He wishes he could capture this on canvas or write it down. A photograph will not do. He knows that this is not possible anyway, so he opens the jam-jar glass window fully and records the whole image for himself, telling his mind not to forget as these moments will never come again, will never be repeated. Not even God Himself can reproduce this moment. It is not just the sight but the smell of woodsmoke and the sounds of scratches in the nearby undergrowth, and the touch of the warm air. He leaves the cigarette to burn to convince himself of the stillness of the day and watches the vortex of smoke filtering through the still air of the room; the taste of tobacco leaf lingers on his tongue.

The ball of fire continues to heat the land and river, disturbing the atmosphere, forming an illusion as heat makes layers of air change density, causing some particles of gas to move more rapidly and into an excited state, colliding with cooler particles as they rise and fall releasing and building electrical charge. Water evaporates and cools as it rises to build clouds which now contain the charge. They become ready to release their stored energy as cloud layers at different temperatures roll over each other creating massive electrical friction reaching down towards the earth's surface. And as the layers rise the storm forms.

Storms here in France are sometimes different to those in Germany. At home they come and go with relative ease and leave the air refreshed. Here the storms can rage all night and day and leave no change to the heat retained in the air. No rain falls and yet the streams the next day will be full and carry on with their work of acting as a reservoir to refresh the land and continue to move the small particles of sand that find their way to the sea.

Heinz has never been to the sea, well not the real sea. This house has seen a thousand of these storms and maybe a thousand more. It has survived, and will go on surviving to see many more thousands in the future.

Heinz watches carefully as it finally rains, large amounts of pear-shaped drops splattering onto the warm, honey-coloured stone of the window sill, at first evaporating instantly with the latent heat stored in the particles of stone. He watches the storm change by the direction of the lightning. Look here, no there, no here. That fast - that quick. He is surrounded by fire from the gods, illuminating the pictures in his room of a family long since gone, ghostly silhouettes of the past, a flash of a flash long forgotten in more ways than one. A man in uniform with his hand placed daringly on her bare shoulder - an unusual familiarity; two very dark, pretty girls, all held in a moment in time, in another time. He has studied the picture well and knows every aspect of it and its frame. He even removed it from the framing once to see if there was a date. As dust swirled everywhere, he thought that the man and woman were probably dead. The heraldry of the uniform betrayed its time. The house perhaps now belonged to the older girl, who would now be very old. Dead too? The teacher perhaps? The owner of the books? The photograph with just a number on the back, written by a travelling photographer and formed in the silver of a room long since gone; like the photographer and his picture of the family. Everything now apparently untraceable.

The falling water now has now released the smells of the warm earth. Tomorrow the grass will be green and perhaps he can return to his park and enjoy just sitting in the warm air. Perhaps, tomorrow, he will stop drinking.

He is thinking of what he can write so he can tell her of his love for her. His mind is clear for once, but he knows that this is a rare moment and may not last. 'My love,' he writes in his mind's eye as it descends towards sleep. 'My love, you are the most wonderful soul I have ever met. You are so gentle and loving. You have only one motive - to love and to be loved in return. I love your challenged innocence and I know you have tried to remain pure for me.' In the morning he will stare at the blank sheets of paper, the unsealed envelope with her name written on it. He will wish he could remember all the loving thoughts he has had the night before, but they will elude him again. It is all so clear and easy when he is on the edge of sleep. He can sleep all day but knows that this will change soon. It is easier to exist in the merciful oblivion of sleep just now.

The first thing he will see when he awakens is his good luck charm of twisted barbs which he will remove from the paper, leaving small particles of iron oxide to be blown off across the table and swirl in the small shaft of light from the hole in the curtains. In his eyes he sees again the thousands falling from the sky, billowing white as they fall to their end. As they shift and move they form a pattern of an image that is well-known to him.

For once he can see her face clearly in the snow-like cloud. It is a small image of great simplicity. She deserves better than him. He needs her to be real, to feel her in that space between head and shoulder created by nature for someone else to place their head as a sign of affection and closeness. It is there for a woman to show that she belongs there and that the man sees this in exactly the same way, too. It is the place that their children will occupy when they need reassurance. He feels his left hand make her shape and her breath makes its way across his chest. The breath is steady as she sleeps, confident in his protective love. This is her place. It is the only place she has ever wanted to be, too.

The breeze moves through the slightly open window and his book falls from his chest. He awakens to realise he has not kept his promise. The brandy bottle lies empty but tells the truth about the taste in his mouth and he knows that when he moves his head will ache. So he sleeps the morning away.

He had selected his fallen book from the many on the library shelves of what had once been a wonderful house, passed down the generations. The French are good at this, he thinks. It is how they retain their dignity. His spoken French has improved so much that he thought he would be able to read quite well. The book is a translation of a work by a very famous English writer. He recognised the writer and the title. It is on the proscribed list. It has been burnt along with the others. The writer was a socialist, who lived and worked long before communism was a dangerous word in any language, but he had not yet read past the first sentence of the book.

*It was the best of times, it was the worst of times, it was the age of wisdom, it was the age of foolishness, it was epoch of belief, it was the epoch of incredulity, it was the season of Light, it was the season of Darkness, it was the spring of hope, it was the winter of despair, we had everything before us, we had nothing before us, we were all going direct to heaven, we were all going direct the other way – in short, the period was so far like the present period, that some of its noisiest authorities insisted on its being received, for good and evil, in the superlative degree of comparison only.*

The words were obviously selected carefully nearly one hundred years ago. They need careful consideration, he believes, if he is to understand the message of the book. He wonders if it means the same in English - such a clever choice of simple words to form such a complicated statement. He wonders what words can fill the empty spectrum between two such words as 'best' and 'worst' - two words that can co-exist at exactly the same time.

The only word he can think of is 'emptiness'. That is how he feels. What he craves is the simplest of times. He does not want light or dark, or even grey. He wants to be able to remember his home and his life as it once was. He wants to go home and back to the woman he knew, and their daughter, back to his life of books; back to books that do not have to be hidden behind other books so that you do not go to prison for reading them.

The strong breeze has finally caught his attention and now he is beneath his tree with two books. The opening pages of the novel lies to one side, face-down on the grass. He has realised that the words are not at opposing ends of anything at all, but are attached and in parallel. They are partners. They occur together. They are in balance, like a finely tuned weighing machine. He could have written, 'It is the best and worst of times', but this does not convey the same meaning. It is not very elegant and would not have attracted the reader. He reads carefully at first, childlike and out loud. He alternates between the book and a dictionary in French and German. He has two unopened letters from his wife, one in each book to mark places, or new words. He will be an old man before he finishes this book. A page is taking fifteen minutes to read as its true meaning is perhaps lost in translation but he is determined to learn this formidable language.

The letters from his wife remain untouched. Her letters have changed. They used to be about love but now she writes as if they are distant friends. If he had opened them he would have noted that she no longer ends her words with a heart and two identical H's within in each other's outline, like the marks you would etch on matching rings for lovers. She speaks briefly of Sophie and their families. She is no longer connected to him. She now just writes, *Hannah*.

\*\*\*

He knows he is in real trouble because he has stopped dreaming, or is it thinking? Just before sleep he forces himself to think of the future with his wife and child. It is a good future where cities and lives are rebuilt. He will design a home for both of them and become a good husband and father. Right now this is not an option. He can no longer hold their faces in his mind, not even for a moment. Their picture appears to be of someone else. He is someone else too. The thought that he will die has never entered his head before, but it has slowly crept in like a thief in the night, smoke under a door, mist in a graveyard. Reality is invading his mind. He has never faced his own death. Not like this. It is eating away within him. He is exhausted but has done nothing to need sleep. Yet he needs to sleep. He can forget everything while he is asleep. Tomorrow everything will be alright. He is more and more isolated. He can go home whenever he wants to, but why bother after the last visit. He loves them both but cannot explain to them or himself why he is this way. He thinks of ways of allowing her to be free of him. He retreats further and further into himself and away from them.

There is a strangeness about being alive. The few older men left from Moscow and Kursk have stopped insulting him. These are his veterans both as comrades and friends. They recognise the signs and close ranks around him. Yes, he reads books, good books, and they know of these books, but cannot even start to read them themselves. He encourages them to read and had passed frozen nights in Russia teaching one of them to read and write. The man's wife has received some beautiful letters from her husband. He has noticed how she is different with him when they are finally taken off the line. He has amazed her by taking them both to the theatre. His confidence with her brings her joy and she responds with warmth and affection; and so it is that Adi has become his great defender. He is a hard man of two World Wars and is not about to allow his friend to fall apart. The banter of the barrack room will have to go elsewhere; Adi makes sure of that. The men of his regiment slowly realise the situation, but as yet no one has an answer to how they might help his health to return.

He is damaged, perhaps beyond repair. The tank battles have shown him what metal can do to metal, flesh and bone, buildings and their contents. The thickest armour cannot protect anyone from a high velocity shell. Crews are often buried together, damaged beyond recognition, inseparable in life and now in death. The tank offers some protection but from this tank there is no protection. This fire burns, it rages like a fever in a small child. There is no answer. He looks at his sidearm, tethered to its holster, hanging over the metal finial of the bed. He looks at the barbed wire still on top of the closed tin box. An accusation of itself as to what is within, what has come and gone, what is now, what may be; everything that there is in the box is himself. As with the neat stack of envelopes next to the decaying tin he can open neither. They will offer no answer. He picks up the sheathed gun and feels the cold steel in his long fingers. There is a simple answer to ending the damage. Instead he pours out a very large brandy and gulps it down. It brings nothing to the fight. He is ashamed. He does not understand how he has got like this and knows that worse is to come.

Adi and the army doctor find him in the attic room, slumped over, awake yet not aware at the small window. The doctor can make a diagnosis without examination. He has seen eyes like this before, eyes that give away their secret of desired death and its close proximity. The mental anguish of one who has seen too much already. The question posed by all soldiers on the battlefield just before life leaves them.

"Why me?"

The doctor has seen it in the trenches of the last war. Men incontinent with fear. Men who shot each other in the leg to avoid facing the inevitable. Men who are unfit for duty and yet consigned to oblivion.

"He should really see someone else - an expert in this field."

Adi slowly shakes his head. "This man is my friend. They would send him back and that would be his final destruction. He is staying here because with your help I will make him well again. I need you to give him time."

A vague thought drifts through the medic's mind. A simple solution is required, but it is risky and not really an answer.

"I will return later."

***

In the evening the local doctor serving the village arrives. He has been sent by the army doctor with an unsigned, hand-written note addressed to 'Adolf'.

*High command has agreed that we can make use of local medical people to help us with the overwhelming number of injured personnel we have to attend to. I think this man has a compression injury to his skull. He needs complete rest. Meanwhile he must cut down on his drinking and you will need to give him the medication I have sent.*

Adi looks at the label and the local doctor reads it for him. Adi has never heard of St John's Wort.

The doctor is content as a physician to be able to assist someone who is so clearly damaged and pleased with the contraband income he can earn, paid in medicines and food, which are in short supply; he will be seen by the Maquis as a useful contact and not as a collaborator. They will expect him to watch and listen.

The old Frenchmen at the cafe have noticed too. They know enough from being soldiers themselves to recognise the signs. They nod wisely as only old Frenchmen can. His sunken eyes and hunched shoulders tell them everything, and if they do not know the coat confirms it. They have seen this before. He is wearing his coat and it is June. They have noted his drinking and smoking. He no longer writes in his little black book or writes letters to his wife at his table in the cafe.

They know he is married, not just by the wedding ring, which he has now removed, leaving an indentation in his finger, but from she who knows everything: the postmistress. He has a daughter too, and they know her name because he writes it on the envelope. Nothing goes unnoticed in these villages, especially by the Dragon. She is the fountain of all knowledge who gives them their pensions as though it is her own money; she listens to every conversation on her small telephone exchange. She is nearly as bad as the Fire who manages the doctor's surgery. The Dragon and the Fire meet each day at the cafe and have long, close-whispered conversations with much shrugging and nodding, but it is the shaking of bowed heads that the old men wait for. This is very important. A wife having an affair, a man in debt to his friend, a farmer who cannot manage anymore, a foreign soldier who is near to the brink in his mind.

"He no longer picks up his mail," she tells her partner in crime. She has stopped him the street to ask him to collect it. It is from your wife, she tells him, such neat writing, but she notices that the letters have become thinner and thinner. They no longer smell of perfume. She is pleased to note that. After all, he is the enemy, even if he is broken beyond repair. Been away too long has that one, she confides to the rumour machine who is sitting opposite her recording everything for later discussion, with her own flavours added. They nod together in smug satisfaction.

When the two women have finished their lunch break the old men order more drinks, count out their change, and wait for Charles to report. For the last hour he has leaned back in his chair pretending to sleep. He is the only one of them who still has good hearing. As a retired gendarme he is able to record the sips of conversation that are interesting, another variation on the truth, but closer than the gossips. He calls it sifting information. The other older men put up with him because he is slightly younger; very boring, but he still has a good short-term memory.

"Well?" A chorus of displeasure. He stalls to allow himself his moment of glory during the days of little entertainment.

"Well Bertrand's wife has got gout and…"

"No. Him. What about him?"

"Who?" More delays. Four unlit pipes with no tobacco in them point at him in unison. A daily occurrence.

"You know very well who." The leader of the pack adds, "Now."

"Your wives have spent all of your money."

"Nothing new there, then. Get on with it."

His report contains very little that is new, but they do not mind recycled news. It is still news. They become very interested when they are told about his letters that are unopened. They are not surprised. His daily routine of drinking coffee and writing has altered. She still writes to letters him, but they are piled up in the post office because he no longer collects them. He has told the doctor that he no longer has the energy to write back.

He would write his letters with materials kept in a leather satchel, which he opens after his first coffee of the day. They were impressed at how he did this each day, and when he sealed the envelope and kissed it they too had feelings of departure, of railway stations and hands waving, kisses of lovers and children, of their own loves once easily expressed when they, too, were that young. The sort of love that is earned, not taken for granted. They noticed how he wrote fluently, his fountain pen - a wedding gift from his wife - held at an unusual angle. He never seemed to correct anything, perhaps the addition of a comma to give clearer meaning; he never seemed to destroy anything. He sometimes wrote in a small black notebook.

At first they thought he was spying on them but they gradually became aware that he was writing in verse. They would nod grudgingly at him at the post office and he would return the greeting with a very formal bow. They noted his injuries and how they appeared to have healed. He looked clean, tidy and fresh-faced. Now he sits with his large brandy accompanied by four equally large empty glasses; a cigarette burns in his hand. The same hand that used to hold the pen now spends its time flicking the cigarette butt or turning the stem of the glass. He gazes into the far distance and no one knows what he is thinking. Now it is time for them to shake their heads. It is not concern that they have for him and yet it sounds very much like a conversation that the old would have about their own children and their children's children. Their thoughts are tinged with a slight sense of guilt. He arrived with physical injury and they quite rightly shunned him when he tried to be friendly. Fraternising with the enemy is forbidden. They would be punished if they appeared to support the occupying force, but this part of France does not feel occupied. Indeed, little has changed. Fraternity is a French notion and it belongs to the French. They sip their drinks and wonder what the force is that is draining this young man.

"Guilt."

"We do not know what he has done."

"He is SS. That is enough explanation."

"He was in Russia."

"How do you know that?"

"The Fire. It is on his medical record."

"Why would he go there and not to his army doctor?"

"Privacy maybe. He only just made it. They were taken off the front line."

"They got hammered in Russia."

"Good for the Russians."

Spit, cough, spit.

"What else?"

"They might end up here one day."

"Who?"

"The Russians."

"No. They would take one look at the Dragon and go home."

"Or try for a doctor's appointment and die from waiting."

Cough, spit, cough. Drink, smoke. Laughter at old jokes.

A black figure appears at the end of the square. No escape. They have been seen. Bravado is the only answer.

"Drink, Father? Smoke?"

"You know I do not do either."

"Nice to see you, Father. How is business?"

"Nice to see you all too. We still have spaces for you at church every Sunday."

"Your church is too damp, Father. We all have lung complaints." A chorus of feigned coughing.

"I am amazed to see that you are all in such good health. It has been such a long time since I have seen you that I thought you were all dead."

"We do not die easily Father."

"No. They say a bad thing is hard to kill." The priest smiles inwardly at his old joke.

"Father, have you seen the tree man?"

"Who?"

"The German." A head nods to the man at the far side of the cafe. "Look, he does not take his coat off on a day like today. He sits under that tree in the field by the river. What do you think, Father?"

"He is at church on Sunday, unlike all of you. He could still save his soul, unlike all of you."

"Think that's what is troubling him?"

"Why?"

"We think he is going crazy. He is not the same. Surely you have noticed, Father."

He has, but this man is not of his flock. Even as a priest he will be treated like any other collaborator if he allows him to be part of his parish. Even Communion on Sunday is difficult. Fortunately, he is always last to receive so everyone can look away and not stand too close. He does not try to make contact so everyone is happy. Why does he not go to the services for the soldiers? He knows the answer to his own question.

"What would you have me do?"

"Nothing, Father; he is the enemy."

"Then why bother me with your stupid questions?"

"We were discussing him when you arrived. You know, just talking."

"Find something better to talk about. Like my roof. You are all still capable of work. Jean, you are a master carpenter. I need new windows."

"More like a new building." Nudges and winks. The presbytery is falling down.

"Are you offering? We could knock it down and rebuild it. I will come and live with you, Young Jacques." He is eighty years old; his father had been Old Jacques. His son, Soldier Jacques, had been killed on the Western Front, leaving him to bring up grandchildren with his daughter-in-law. Jacques had ceased to be a family name.

"You still know how to dress stone don't you, Jacques?"

"It would take him all day to set one stone."

"That's nearly as long as it takes him to pee."

Laughter, cough, smoke, drink. Wheeze, polite choking. Priests still counted for something.

"It won't be long before some of you come to my church, head first and carried in and out in your boxes."

The last time Young Jacques was in a church was when they had buried his son. He knew it was an empty coffin weighed down with stone. The spirit stays and his wife is content. She goes to church every day, for both of them, he jokes, but it is really to see her son. He finds no comfort there.

"You should be ashamed of yourselves." Heads bowed; little boys again.

"Yes, Father."

"What poor examples you are."

"Yes, Father. We are."

The priest turns away and smiles to himself. These are proud men in the autumns of their years and they have brought up good children. They are proud of their achievements. They are friends with God and He with them, even if they do not visit Him very often. In their prime they were the first to offer when help was needed. They have carried their elders to their resting places, rebuilt the church after the great storm, paid for the bell, dug graves for the poor and took no payment unless it could be afforded.

He smiles again to himself, satisfied that France is still in good hands. There will always be such old men as these, everywhere. He does not even wince as a very pretty girl passes by on a bicycle, her dress billowing in the self-created slipstream, showing long, shapely legs; encouraging whistles and slightly raucous laughter. Well, most of France is in good hands. A sermon for Sunday: the continuity of the Great Plan. Even old men and certainly pretty girls are part of His plan.

"Hey, Father. That's your bike she is riding."

It disappeared a few weeks ago as she now does, turning the corner, neither girl nor machine to be seen again. Too late now to give chase, in spite of the encouraging comments from his congregation at the cafe.

***

The not-so-young girl on the borrowed bike is one of the first to know. The message is imprinted in her brain. She thinks she knows what it means and has a good story to cover her movements. It is her birthday tomorrow. She will be twenty years old. She was born in the early hours of 6 June 1924. Her birthday celebrations will never be the same again.

The Dragon and the Fire have gone. So has the priest; the soldier has gone to his tree with his books and cigarettes ; the cafe front passes into shadow and, like actors, one by one they leave their stage in silence, nodding their farewells to each other. There will be much to talk about tomorrow. They will all be back to greet the start of a new day, except the soldier. He will be summoned by a higher authority. The old men will not see him again at the cafe.

The house greets him like an old, drunken friend who has lost his way. He could bring Hannah and Sophie here. When this is over he will return with them. They could sit at the cafe and finally have a conversation with the locals because by then they would have won. They would be free and Germany would be defeated. He could show Sophie his tree and the small river which is not really much more than a stream. They could stand on the bridge and watch the old men fishing for their supper. If the house is available they could share it and he will be able to explain to his wife how he reached this point in his life. He realises he needs to explain everything to everyone.

He pauses at the door, one hand searching for keys, the other steadying himself on the warm stonework. The door is slightly open, just revealing the marks from winter's swelling of ancient timbers. He always checks it two or three times whenever he leaves. He remembers seeing an old woman doing the same. She would return from the tram stop to check that she had locked her house. He simply keeps his keys in the same pocket to tell himself that he has closed the door properly. It is a danger, an open door. It can mean a trap. He pushes it open further with an extended foot. He is not armed. He is barely in uniform. He has not shaved for days. No one ever really checks on him, except Adi and the doctor. They know where he is and that is made even clearer when he sees the envelope waiting for him above the fireplace. He recognises the writing too. They have sent his friend to summon him back to the war. A war that has moved far away for him.

He puts down the letter he received that morning at the strangely silent Post Office. The Dragon served him but even her usual manner had been off hand. The whole population just stared at the floor as many of them were in the triangle that is called the village square. There were no boule players or old men at the cafe. At first he wondered if perhaps it was closed but there was Henri, half-way through the door, polishing a glass but concentrating on something happening inside. The whole village seemed to be present inside the bar but there was little conversation. Indeed there were none of the high-pitched greetings usual on other fine mornings. He took his letter in exchange for the one he had finally written to his wife. He stares at her letters as he places the new one with the rest, which are unopened. For the first time in months he has a decision to make; brandy or Adi's letter. He opens the letter. Brandy will take second place for a long time to come.

The scratchy writing is clear. They have sent a car for him and he is to return to HQ immediately. He understands the message from his friend as he adds 'Be ready at 1100 hours tomorrow. They're back. Here we go again.' A comment they use to greet each other with before they go into battle. The note is signed and dated, *Adi S. 06.06.1944. 3 p.m.*

He picks up his other mail and goes to his room. He opens and reads Hannah's letters in the order sent and packs them in the dust-covered suitcase. Each of his actions seem to help him clear his mind of the cobwebs of being unable to face life, as he now realises that he will once again return to the only fear a soldier has: how to face death.

*** 

"Where were you yesterday? You missed everything. They're back."

"Nice of you to ask. I am fine, how are you? What did I miss? Who is back?"

"Sorry. I am fine. All hell broke loose yesterday and we are moving out to Normandy."

"Normandy?"

"The invasion. It has come and they chose Normandy. No one can understand why but that's the Allies for you. Makes no sense. How do you supply an army across that distance?"

"What is the current position?"

"As far as we know we are holding them near the beaches and they are in trouble. But they must be mad. Such a distance to cross. How do you get tanks and armour across miles of ocean?"

"Where are we going now?"

"We have a few local problems to sort out before we can go north. One of our senior officers has been captured by the Maquis. We have to get him back, no tanks for you yet, Major."

"I am not a major."

"No, but you soon will be, at the rate we are losing senior officers."

"Do we know who the officer is?"

"Yes."

"Are you sure they have him?"

"All of him. Or not, as may be."

"Who is in charge of the operation?"

"Our old friend."

"Please tell me you are joking."

"No, sir."

"That man spells trouble for anyone. They are friends. He will spare nothing and nobody to find him; dead or alive. I fear what that man will do if he is not restrained. I have seen him in action before."

"Yes, sir. We both have."

# PART THREE

"Come to bed. It is nearly midnight."

"No. We have been chosen. We are the first."

"Come to bed," insists Madame Gondree to her husband. It is rare that he ever receives such an invitation from his wife, and certainly never twice. He knows he is tired but events are about to take place that he wishes to either witness or be part of. This is the most important night of his life; sleeping is not an option. This is the most important night for all of France.

"I must watch. I may be able to help. We will be needed before this night is through."

He is sitting outside his cafe; everything of importance in the world is just behind him; his business, his wife, a small daughter asleep. Both are unaware of the fact that right now above the coast of France are thousands of men whose thoughts he cannot comprehend. He tries to think of how they may feel when they land to face the Germans nearby. He has been fortunate. The Germans used his cafe and business has been good. He has made a profit out of them being here but this will end soon. The British are coming. He has been told that the drop zone will be nearby. Just how near is to surprise even him.

He puffs impatiently on his pipe, covering the glowing embers, warming his time-worn hands and shading the red glowing embers of light. He so wanted to be part of this but he cannot stay awake and tiredness is going to deprive him of his objective. The silence of his dreams is penetrated by the hissing noise of fast moving objects splintering their way through the lightly-packed summer air. It sounds like air escaping from an inflated bicycle tyre, only louder, followed by dry wood breaking, cracking like a whiplash as if burning in the open grate, and then voices he cannot understand.

"We need your assistance m'sieu. We have wounded." The voice and hand of a British Soldier shakes him awake.

His alertness surprises him.

"*Le cav; suivez-moi.*" They have arrived and he missed it. His wife appears with a startled young daughter, who is smiling at the men with blackened faces. He beckons them to the cellar door.

"Where is everyone? You cannot beat the Germans with ten men and two of them wounded."

"We've come to take the bridge." Stuttering French suddenly matches the gunfire outside.

"With so few?"

"There are more of us outside."

They are really here and he knows now by the chaos outside that they are here in some force. There are no human voices, only actions with small arms fire, large, heavy-calibre fire, machine gun, mortars firing, taking a short arc to their targets, exploding and then total silence.

Minutes later it is over and the first part of France to be liberated is in the hands of the British and his house is full of armed soldiers. He starts to weep.

'*Liberté,*' he thinks. 'The most powerful of words in any language.'

He is pleased that they are British; had not his father spoken proudly of how they had fought together in the Great War? Once again they have come to the aid of France, perhaps enemies of old, but now united in one cause: the defeat of Nazism.

"Sir, we have the bridge."

"Well done."

"Sir, Lt. Brotheridge did not make it."

"Damn."

"We have more wounded sir, but the Germans have stopped firing."

"Hold positions. Do not engage further. We have our target. Bring the wounded here. Tell everyone else to hold their positions and await further instructions. Do not fire without cause."

The major turns to the owner of the cafe.

"I will need your cellar."

"*Absoluement.*"

"And a large brandy."

"*Absoluement.*"

Frank is already unloading his medical supplies in the cellar. He had wanted to be among the first back in France. As he begins to set a soldier's leg, which looks broken Madame Gondree arrives with another woman.

"Medic." She points at her friend. "Infirmiere." She starts to move her fingers over the soldier's leg. The ankle is sprained. There is no broken leg. She leaves them to deal with a bullet wound in the arm.

"You are so few," the cafe owner's wife says to no one in particular.

"This is just the start." Frank looks at his watch. It has taken them ten minutes to achieve their objective. The next five hours will be the longest night of their lives. "There are thousands more on the way - hundreds of thousands, on boats and planes. They are already clearing the beaches and falling from the sky."

"You may stay, but the rest of you out. Go somewhere else, we need the cellar." She looks at Frank and they start to unpack the rest of his medical kit. The soldiers, who have slim hopes for a cup of tea, file out; no one argues with Mme Gondree, but she smiles to herself because news they have waited for four years is finally here. The liberation of France is now underway. Frank takes the opportunity to take a small card from his pocket with the names of seven dead children written upon it and tucks it into the corner of the wooden frame of the simple menu outside the Gondree Cafe.

*\*\*\**

No one argues with Mother Superior either - another formidable French Woman. As she watches the girl from the confines of her office, her concern for their adopted daughter is self-evident. Months have passed and Lucy has barely communicated. She can carry out all the tasks they give her and the doctor confirms that there is no mental damage, but still she does not speak of anything that passed before she arrived here.

The Reverend Mother can see the walled garden clearly from her office window, and in the middle of the neat rows of vegetables, the slim figure of a very lovely young woman. It is clear now that she is just that, her dark facial features framed by strands of unruly hair. She watches her push the loose curls into the headscarf. They will have to bring in one of the village girls to do something with her hair. Even a Reverend Mother can see what a young man would find beautiful in Lucy, despite those badly fitting second-hand clothes. They will miss her when she leaves them; the other sisters see her as one of their own and yet not as a nun or novitiate. They all have a younger sister now.

Lucy stands up straight, aware somehow that she is being watched over by an uncritical eye. She smiles; she has grown to love this place of peace and flowers and well-tended vegetable gardens, and above all the patience and security, the love and kindness that the sisters show her. Before she starts work each day she walks around as if checking that the high walls are still there and stops at the locked gates. She waits there and gazes along the road that brought her here. She, too, is aware that she is different, yet she follows the same code as the nuns and rarely leaves the convent, increasingly so after one of the young market boys tried to engage her in conversation. She is happy in this sheltered environment and wants no other. When Reverend Mother suggested she should be in a foster home with new parents and a family she had screamed so much that the nuns working on the placement gave their senior good advice. She knows that they do not want her to go either. She brings a quality to the place that no one else can. In the early months her screams were the only sound that she made apart from humming along at evensong, but that had gradually subsided. No one wishes a return of those nightmares for the girl.

***

Convents are run on very tight rules. Bells for this and that, for breakfast, lunch and evening meals. But the most important bells are the ones that call the nuns to prayer. Since the occupation, the outside church bell has not been rung even for Sunday Mass. When the rhythms of this life are disturbed it can be catastrophic. News of the invasion comes while they are at prayer. France is still mostly asleep at the time of the 6 a.m. Angelus, and interrupting prayer is usually unthinkable. Reverend Mother gives a pretention of being annoyed but the news has come through by clandestine radio; and this is about prayers that have been answered.

"Normandy," the sisters whispered to each other after Reverend Mother called for a special day of consideration and prayer for a successful outcome.

"They have come," she tells the small congregation. "Some of own boys have returned to their own soil. We may be needed again. We must do an inventory of medical and food supplies and bring out the old blankets that we collected from the town. Our skills will be needed again."

"Yes, Reverend Mother."

"Bring Lucy to me. She will be at the gate, no doubt."

"Yes, Mother."

"And ring the church bell. The rest of France should know right now."

***

The midday sun is hot the day they arrive. The south walls of the village have already absorbed much of the morning heat, keeping their residents cool. The church walls have been moving slowly outwards since the day the bell was put into place - very small movements that no one ever notices. The west wall in the strong summer sun expands faster than the east wall, which is mostly in the shade. This village is used to slow imperceptible change and it wants this to continue.

They arrive in their trucks and cars. You can hear the harsh clip of their jack-boots, ticking and tacking in unison on the smooth stone sets as they march down the main street, foreboding vibrations never heard before in this village. Some of them arrive a little later, on foot with a small group of local farmers and their wives; their ancient homes are still burning. They are made to stop in the market square as the villagers are ordered from their homes. Others are hiding nearby, witnesses for what is to come. The market place has been there for a thousand years and more. It is the original place the first inhabitants used for trade after the first soldiers went back home. Their lives and dreams are still connected to the stones they moved here to make their first camp fires. Small amounts of their spent fuel are still in the dust that makes up the earth of this place. And although the embers of the fires that are their lives are long-since extinguished, not everything about them has been forgotten.

Human beings are so fortunate. When they sleep they escape to another world, which can also be sometimes troubled, but it is always different, at least. They can slip from one world to another, altering it as they go, not always dreaming, or in control of their thoughts, but sometimes seeking understanding. They can separate, divide and unite their thoughts. As they become older they sometimes forget things until the sleep and forgetfulness join and everything ends. For this village it just goes on and on, and continues to do so. The memories reach back hundreds of years, but in the silence of their nights, when humans are at peace and childlike in my care, the memories continue.

Sometimes they miss the most amazing things of all: the animals that only play at night; the closeness of contented lovers in the dark sleeping securely in each other's arms; the planets and stars moving across the heavens; the incandescent debris which, pulled in by gravity, falls from space, leaving a glow in its final path as it accelerates to oblivion. The village is not allowed this silence because everything about everyone is remembered, but there are things which this village would prefer to forget, like the day the soldiers come. The day its nightmare starts and the dreams end.

Without warning they are everywhere. In every building of this village they are searching, shouting and screaming, rounding up my people as if they are criminals.

When he arrives at the hotel he does not wait for his new driver to guide him from the car. He practically rips the door from its hinges as he rams it open outside the old *Hôtel Avril*. He is thinking about a particular abduction a few days ago. His friend and fellow officer was killed by these savages. There are Jews living here too. He can smell them. They are probably all Jews here anyway, or sympathisers. He is so angry. They dared to do this. They are trying to stop the greatest fighting machine in the world. And the Americans have finally arrived and are in a need of a good hiding too. Another nation run by Jews and Jew lovers, and here he is, stuck with rounding up the remnants of the Maquis who dare delay him from the real fight, dared to kill his friend, his comrade in arms; they dared, this scum.

"Search the hotel." His recently appointed driver, Heinz, nods and enters the small hotel. The SS officer begins to walk towards the villagers, who are gathered together in the little area that they call the Fair Ground, but this is not like a market day. The usual joyous noises are missing. There is no squeezing of fruit and shaking of heads. No semi-ribald comments from the butchers. No one is buying anything. The children are with their mothers, but none of them asks for bon-bons. There is a different smell that day, a smell that has been described since the dawn of time as the smell of death.

The men of the village are separated from the women and children. This is worrying. It is not the way things happened before. They can feel it in the atmosphere around them. The men and some older boys are taken to a barn, the women and the rest of their families to the church. A passing group of cyclists looking for a cafe are taken to a garage and told to wait. A tram arrives but it is sent on its way; no one is allowed to disembark.

\*\*\*

I am unable to bear witness. I am only a village, but every event and all your memories that occur here are recorded. I know that my stones vibrate when his name is shouted clearly by the SS trooper carrying a large black box. He is furious that his name is used. Names are rarely used and never on a mission like this.

The stones of this village absorb his name. They hide it away in the centre of their atoms to remain there for all time. The vibrations of that sound can still be sensed now. It is a name that will be remembered here forever. A record of the venom of one man. The head teacher of the school has also heard his name. He is now pushing her, with his handgun in her back, towards the church to be with her teachers.

"What are you doing?" she asks him in perfect German.

"Searching for Maquis."

"There are none here. Just old men, women and children."

"Then they will do."

"This is a peaceful village. We even have some of your fellow countrymen living here."

"They are not true Germans."

His eyes keep searching. A shallow, sunken face with a long jaw bone, his customary shaved head magnifying his Aryan appearance, eyes set deeply in thin skin. Eyes searching for witnesses.

She speaks to him again. She makes the same mistake as the young officer, her voice perfectly pitched as any teacher's at an assembly naming a naughty child. It echoes from the entrance to the church.

"They will find you. All of you."

The church door slams shut in front of her as a single shot echoes around the empty square. George's mother dies on the church steps.

The older children begin to weep and the women start to scream. Men's voices and more shots, strange hissing noises and men screaming in high pitched agony. A smell like no smell ever before. A Jewish mother hiding in the village knows the smell of burning human flesh. Surely after everything she has been through with her children, who are hiding in the *Hôtel Avril*, it is not going to end like this. She begins to pray. They all begin to pray. They all know.

The windows of the church crash inwards as bullets crack the frescoed ceilings and walls, destroying the list of the names of the honoured dead from the Great War. The large black box appears to move slightly. From the outside the church expands and then contracts. Human noise from within stops. In the explosion small bodies are vaporised instantly. Mothers watch their babies disappear as they, too, are overcome by the searing heat of expanding gases. The walls are hot and wet and covered with the remains of the people.

I can show you exactly where on my walls every drop of their most precious blood fell. They are still there now. The tower begins to burn. The children by the great altar may have watched two women and a baby escape from the damaged windows and fall to their freedom behind the church, but not even their mothers covering them with their own bodies can prevent their deaths, too. As the older escapee crawls to hide in the vegetable garden behind the church, she sees the mother and her crying baby being silenced with single gunshots. The main doors of the church fly open, briefly showing a few more survivors, their village burning. They see the burnt bodies of grandfathers in protective embraces with their grandsons and sons. A machine gun ends the futile attempted escape from the church and their vision of what is becoming their hell. An SS Officer shoots another screaming baby through the head. The mother dies with the same bullet. As the shooting begins to stop, the burning increases, and a badly burned but still breathing body lies perfectly still in the undergrowth, unaware that she is one of the few survivors. The world should take the warning that there are always survivors to an atrocity, no matter how big or small, and sometimes they are the most unexpected of witnesses.

***

In the church a little boy is screaming for his dead mother. Heinz looks at her burnt hands and face. The little boy is very close to death. He has been sent in here by his commander who is aware that his driver is close to his own self-destruction. He has no time for weakness in anyone, even well-respected, previously decorated soldiers.

"Finish them off. I will return to check," he commands his driver as he departs, satisfied that the main task is over.

Heinz looks at the once-pretty, dark-haired woman with a scarlet ribbon around her neck. At some time earlier this day she had brushed her hair carefully and tied it back with the same colour of ribbon; perhaps her husband is coming home to lunch and she had wanted to look her best for him. Who knows? She is holding something tightly in her fingers. Heinz pulls gently on the scarlet ribbon to allow three gold rings to escape, one by one, her dead fingers momentarily taking on the appearance of life again. One of the rings is a simple gold wedding band, like the gold in the rocks beneath this church. He raises his head to see the grasping leeches stealing from the dead mothers and raises his gun at the same time.

"Get out," he orders the blood-suckers and fires a shot at them - the first shot he has fired today. They leave like ghouls, their grasping hands empty of booty. He cuts the ribbon on either side of the woman's broken neck and ties the ends together. He buries the rings and its scarlet necklace in the protective rubble by the altar. He gently slides the remaining scrap of ribbon from behind her shattered spine and does not know why but he puts it into his breast pocket, leaving a small piece of the scarlet ribbon showing in the rubble, trusting the next visitor to this destroyed place will try to find their rightful owner.

He arrives in the church, ready to carry out his own orders. He is about to shoot the dying boy but Heinz does not allow him the satisfaction of such a deed and the accusations that might follow; he closes his eyes and does it himself - a kindness of sorts. A look of pure hatred passes between himself and his jealous, less decorated senior officer. Heinz thinks about the final rounds in his gun but would rather save them for himself. Rather that than face a firing squad of his own soldiers. He considers some form of retribution, but for what? What has this man actually done? And then he is distracted by further German voices shouting outside the church. He leaves Heinz with a final order:

"Go back and check the hotel again." Still looking for a way to catch him out.

***

Oradour burns.

It burns easily. It does not need the fuel that they add. Ancient timbers dried by time crack and groan in their own death throes; furniture, lovingly waxed by years of polishing, being passed down from mother to daughter, burns. Family heirlooms, boxes of books and small wooden toys made by grandfathers all burn, adding to the impression that this is the end of time. Roofs fall inwards, sucking window frames and doors into the fires. Houses explode as high octane fuel is sprayed through windows. Photographs curl in the heat, their images turning back to the silver and nitrogen from which they were made. The photographs of the children so recently taken in the school and proudly presented by the children to parents and grandparents as though they had made the image themselves, they burn too.

These are images of the same children who marched quietly to the church in their ranks like soldiers. The older ones had known that it was not a holy day that came later in the month. The younger ones would have made their First Holy Communion on that day and the village would have been especially decorated in their honour. They would have had breakfast in the school hall and the school would have been closed. They would have all played late in the Fair Ground and had a picnic, usually provided by grandparents. These were the children who had walked down past the tram stop to where the Germans were waiting.

Oradour continues to burn. Oak which seeded itself over a thousand years ago burns, but it resists, waiting out the baking heat. It will remember. It seals itself so that the air cannot penetrate its fibres. The ancient timbers do not fall into the inferno. They have no intention of going just yet. They will still be here in another thousand years, evidence and testimony for all time. The wood grows harder; it will be difficult to remove the evidence of certain explosives and metal shards, which have penetrated the resins which coat their surfaces, leaving evidence of where they were made. They are still there to this day and they wait. Evidence, if anyone ever needs it, to tell the world who was responsible for this crime - yet another witness to be called.

\*\*\*

The south-facing front of the *Hôtel Avril* has few windows in the guest rooms as it takes the midday heat and in the late afternoon casts a long shadow over the open fields towards the dense wood and the cemetery. It remains undamaged at first, until wisps of smoke appear everywhere, especially at the upper windows. A small, frightened face appears at one of the open widows, followed by two more. The roof is now engulfed in flames as a small boy is pushed out of a first floor window, followed by two older children. The fact that there are three souls hiding in the back bedrooms does not seem to bother them at all. They must have heard the little one cry out. It is clear enough for everyone. His screams are still heard the following day. How will anyone know what took place here? The soldiers are laughing and joking with each other as they set fire to the hotel.

"Frenchmen burn better than Russians."

"No they don't. They are full of smelly cheese, not vodka."

"Or anti-freeze."

"French villages burn better. Good wood."

These men are not out of control. They have burned other places, too, and their officers are busy ensuring that the orders are carried out, but they are unaware that there are survivors and the very man they have come to find is still alive nearby. They do not see three figures in the shadow of the hotel escaping across the fields, but Heinz does. He has gone to the rear of the hotel to vomit. The village can hear that terrible noise humans make when they reverse their eating process. Some of the others have been drinking covertly with wine stolen from the wine shop. A few of them have drunk too much and are also being sick, but this is not the same. He has no fever and has had no alcohol since his return to duty. He is walking across the field at the back of the hotel, looking for a place where he does not have to be part of this when he sees three figures moving towards him. He turns quickly to see a young, dark-haired woman and two children. The small boy is coughing and crying. His eldest sister picks him up. She has spent the day reassuring him that they will find their parents soon and that she will take care of them. She has told them to be quiet and so they are; there is no record of their whispers. There are only the sounds or the reports of voices. They were heard jumping from the window. The older girl screams as the soldier shouts. There are three gunshots and a man's voice softly telling them to run. His voice and the sounds of his firing are absorbed by the nearby buildings that are still left. No one else hears his final command - the walls make sure of that. His order remains locked in the particles that form the wall behind the hotel. It is still locked in there.

"That way," he commands them. "Go to the woods." He points his gun along the rapidly disappearing shadows of the now-burning hotel.

Two sets of feet pummel the ground and then there is silence. If anyone has observed he will be dead too. But the walls protect him from sight and let him vomit in privacy, everything he has done is known only to the village walls. Three more have survived as witnesses; two girls and a small boy with a damaged ankle.

He is now finished and does not look for his driver. He has more urgent business further north. He is well satisfied with everything he has done, including leaving his driver behind. The Maquis will not bother them anymore. Everyone takes their lead from him, except Heinz, who is left behind at the hotel as rumour spreads that the Maquis are nearby. He is still being sick when the first of them arrive.

*** 

Georges reads the copy of the radio message from Polish Toni with tired eyes. There are only two people who know of his exact whereabouts. Messages are only sent if there is a real emergency. The message is simple: "Your car is in the garage." He has to return to Oradour. It is not that far but it means postponing the next attack. He watches from a church tower as a group of unknown German troops pass through a village. He is not aware of expected troop movements nearby. His company of the Marquis has been moving to the west of Limoges, leaving the garrison town untouched. He has explained to his men and women that this is a way of stopping reprisals. They have control of the roads. The Germans are having to fight their way through every kind of obstacle that can be found. A tree felled across the road costs an hour, a burnt-out wagon thirty minutes. A blown bridge is at least a day. They are making life difficult for the enemy, but his orders are to kill no one. He has insisted on this so that there will be no reprisals.

*** 

As they arrive at Oradour Georges notices the small group of men standing together at the side of the road; they are silhouetted by what looks like the sunset, but the light is coming from the wrong direction. Toni waves to his man to pull the ancient farm wagon over. He opens the window and the smell hits him. A smell he does not recognise amongst others that he knows well. Georges looks at him, a face that tells of dread looks back. The small group divides and allows him to pass to the rise. He is greeted by a scene of devastation from the First World War. The village is burning.

"The Germans came," says Toni, standing next to Georges. "We were too late."

"How many?"

"About two hundred men."

"No. How many did they kill?"

"Everybody. Men, women, children, babies."

"My family."

A nod.

"Survivors?"

"Some children. One or two others."

***

You have to know this:

I tried, I really did. I have seen death before. In this village it is usually a gentle passing. A slight breeze, perhaps a sigh, maybe some tears, and a good soul is swept away. This is different. They will not go. I try to tell them, I really do, but they are not listening. I try to heal them, to make them feel whole again, and send them on their way, but they are like me, destroyed. And I am haunted by their souls. There is no one left to grieve for my dead. They are alone. Many of them even I cannot recognise. They are burnt beyond recognition, but I still know them as my own. For days they still go about their previous lives. The children still go to school, complain that it is summer and that they have homework to do before they can play. They wait for the final bell that will end the summer term, but it never sounds. They go home to their mothers, whose bodies still lie in the church, as they do. They still kiss each other goodnight, but there are no smiles and no re-assurances.

Then Georges arrives. I know immediately. He is one of my oldest friends. He walks into what is left of his home. I can feel his agony and despair. You would have made the same judgement. This man is on the edge, perhaps even beyond it. He could have done anything. His friend, Polish Toni, has a restraining hand on a sleeve.

"Don't," he says.

Georges pulls himself free. "Where are they?"

"Your mother is on the steps of the church. Your wife and boy are inside."

He walks up the steps to the burnt-out church. He covers his mother's body with his coat and enters the church. His screams are louder than those who have died. In fact there are no words to describe them. When he comes out someone has removed his mother's body.

"What shall we do?" his friend asks, offering him a bottle of uncorked brandy.

"Do we know where they are? Do we know who they are?"

"Of course. We even have a name."

"Then follow them and keep contact."

"What then?"

"We will kill them. Kill them all. They have taken everything." This man is not recognisable anymore. What is left of the walls feel the chill in his words and the death of his soul.

What happens next will remain forever in my memory.

\*\*\*

The villagers suddenly assemble in the Fairground just as they did when the soldiers came. They are mostly the mothers with their children, and the old folks and some young men. A group of accidental passing cyclists is there too. They are all smiling now and the children are playing.

"Have you all brought your pencils and crayons? Don't forget you still have work to do." How do I forget this? All the women, all the mothers, and all of those who are about to be mothers, and those who never now will be - they are all there. They are as beautiful as I remember them on their very best of days. They look perfect. They are perfect, the men and boys too. They are all in their Sunday best. Their white shirts bring a particular brilliance of purity that men only seem able to bring to complement a bride on her wedding day. A memory of when their lovers wore white too? Perhaps they are not so pure but their love for each other is. Be assured of that. Young girls in short white socks giggle and laugh in a way boys never quite understand. The boys think of fishing with their grandfathers, or building secret dens in the woods - places that the girls had no wish to go to.

The young doctor is there, too. He is standing by his burnt-out car with his black medical bag in his hand. He looks as if he is going to his surgery and then speaks very clearly. I think he is going to say, 'next, please,' but he frowns and speaks different words.

"Alright everyone, it is time."

The mayor checks his broken watch and nods. They all look up at the church clock. It has stopped at 4 p.m.

There is a sense of relief when they start to leave. It is the same feeling as when a storm has passed overhead and the lightning conductors have done their job and the thunder reveals itself in the distance, and worried parents sleep again on a warm summer's night; or when a small child wakes in the morning after having had a high temperature all night and their mother, sitting in the chair next to their bed, wakes with relief when they hear their child speak.

"Mummy, I am hungry."

But it is nothing like that. The mother knows that her sick child will be out playing again as soon as they have eaten, but none of these children will ever know what play is again. I guess I am selfish, but I cannot go on like this. I have to let them go. I have to make them go.

Long grasses are now hiding the scuffed shoes of boys running boldly to the front; satchels on their backs empty now save their pencils and crayons. At the back a small boy holds hands between his grandma and mama. He swings on their arms.

"Again," he pleads. "Again."

The little boy's mother turns to look back at her village. She was born here. It is her village. She does not want to go anywhere else. This is her home. It has always been her home. I remember her being born here. The old doctor delivered her. It was a difficult birth. Her mother had waited for three days for her baby daughter to survive and then her spirit left us. Her place is still marked and loved in one of the special fields of carved stones and crosses.

The little boy shouts, "Nana, mama, once more, please." Everyone else has now passed beyond the tree line, a boundary in time set forever. His mother is still looking back. She smiles.

She taps the side of her head and points towards the church where she was married. She points to her temple - or is it to her eyes? - then to her heart and finally to her lips. She touches her lips and lingers there to blow a final kiss to a lover, or a friend she knows she will not see again; perhaps even to me. She makes a fist with her right hand and strikes her breast three times. She knows she is going away. She points to the church again and her lips move. Her whisper vibrates through my stones, a shiver that will be recorded forever. I can still feel her words now, her gentle words:

"Remember me. Remember us. Remember them and what they did to us."

Then they are gone and I cannot see them anymore.

"One last time mamma, nana, one last time."

The joyful laughter of a small boy, a faint hissing noise of foliage rasping on foliage, grass whipping on grass, seeds falling, air sighing on its way through the vents created by nature, a vortex that sweeps away the essence of my being.

And then the incredible silence replaced by a violent disturbance as someone awakens from an induced sleep.

\*\*\*

Our shared dream ends. I cannot make things happen but I can allow thoughts to flow. Neither of us is at peace. I allow him the only memory I can. He sees his mother smiling, his son playing, his wife waving and pointing. Her message to him is clear. 'See my love for you. How do I love thee? Three times I love thee; with my heart, with my very breath, with my very soul.' I let him remember one final intimate memory he has of his wife. It is one that I will never share with anyone else.

A distant echo of a Polish voice passes through the awakening.

"They are coming back. We must go. We must leave here."

A black, cloaked hoard descends onto the church steps. They start to try to cleanse the village. They dig a large trench behind the church and many of the dead are moved there. They work quickly and methodically but are making no real impact. Their loud, moaning voices carry to the edge of the village beyond the church. The ghouls have returned.

He watches at a distance and decides not to kill them; he knows he can't even when some of the villagers are thrown down a well. His dream will not clear from his mind. It is still in the crossover point where she said goodbye. He is unwilling to allow the sensation to disappear. He does not want them to clear away the body of his son and wife. He wants to do this himself. He does not want the murderers back in his village. But he knows he must stay hidden and wait.

The sounds of distant battle halts all activity. They return to the steps of the church, fall in and board their trucks. They leave. A simple tactic of staging a fire fight a few miles away, mostly involving fireworks, had worked again. They fall for it every time. These troops have the jitters. They know it is over, but they do not want to be caught by the Maquis. They know what will happen to them, especially now. There will be no prisoners taken.

As soon as they go the very same Maquis begin to cover bodies with clean white sheets. Georges takes two sheets into the church for his wife and son but their bodies have already been removed by his friends. His son's body had been just in front of the altar, his wife just in front of her son, forming herself around him in a protective shield. Many of the women are in a similar position, protecting their children. He stands at the spot and places the sheets on the ground. He kneels, but prayer is beyond him now and always will be. In the rubble of what was once the main altar a thin scarlet ribbon curls its way through the broken masonry. He recognises it as her favourite colour and gently pulls it clear. There are three rings on it. He places the ribbon around his neck, feeling the weight of her rings - his rings. Now he knows why she was pointing at the church. He holds her wedding ring and their betrothal ring, which he had bought as a sign of his love. The third ring he had bought because she liked it and because she had told him of the need to start building a new bedroom.

Outside, other men in blue overalls are arriving with shrouds to bury the dead and catalogue the crime. They do not have a shroud large enough to cover this dying village.

Georges is aware that earlier he captured a very important German officer. This is actually the last thing he needs right now. They did not plan for prisoners. This officer is different. He is important. He is sitting in the next room, under armed guards with instructions to shoot him if he moves. They let his driver go with a very special message about trading prisoners for his precious hostage.

The door to the room is open. Georges' prisoner is sitting with his back to the doorway. He is looking out of the window at the destroyed village. The distant blue sky forces an ancient memory to form in his mind's eye. He thinks about the holidays of his childhood and his family back in Germany. So far they are safe. He remains motionless as Georges enters the room of what had been the upper floor of a house. They had brought him here so that he would see and know what had taken place. It is the fact that he is still alive and knows he can be traded for captured Maquis that gives him hope. He is a soldier and he took no part in this. They know that.

"Your soldiers did this."

"Do you know who I am?"

"Everyone in this village has been murdered."

"Let them pass. Why did you not let us pass? We were only defending ourselves."

"And we are only defending our country; killing unarmed innocent women and children is not defending yourself."

The German Officer stares at him. "You killed these people. You caused this. The Resistance brought this on their own people by attacking us. Reprisals were ordered. We follow orders. We are needed in Normandy. There is no need for any of this."

"You are quite correct, but you see, this is my village and my country, not yours. You were never invited here and when you have all left we will…" Georges is looking out of the window. Small bodies are being removed from behind the altar in the church. A child's hand falls from under the white sheet and is quickly covered again. The body is placed next to that of an adult woman that had been near it in the church.

"Stand up and take a look at your achievements. You must be very proud of what you have done. What did your Fuhrer promise you; a thousand years? All this in just over a thousand days - what an achievement."

"I played no part in this. I was not here. I did not give any orders. I am a prisoner of war. I demand the right to be treated accordingly. I take it you have heard of the Geneva Convention?"

"What has taken place here is a crime."

"I demand my rights."

Georges looks to the doorway and nods to Toni, his only real friend. "You have no rights. Take him away."

Georges watches the scene from the window. "If you had just apologised, said you were sorry."

Georges calls his senior Maquis leaders to Oradour.

"This is why we fight; this why men are dying on the beaches and fields of Normandy. Men who are not of our nation have come to our aid and so we must help them. We must do everything to assist them in our fight. We must change now, and fight back, like a true army. This is why we resist, because when everything else in gone, our freedom, our wives, our children, and our fellow countrymen on the transport trains, when they have murdered everyone, all we have is this chance to resist. There is nothing else left for good men to do. We need to find the men who destroyed this place - find all of them and destroy them. They are in our country and they have no right to be here. They have no right to do this. They have lost their right to life. Our people did nothing to deserve this. My mother, my wife and son - your wives and children, our fathers and mothers - did nothing to deserve to die like this. This is an evil which will only be destroyed by the fire itself. That is what they fear the most, you know, the fire that we will create just for them. They must all die in the same way they have brought upon our villages. Oradour, Tulle… all must be accounted for, but first we have a job to do. The supply column that is heading north to assist Das Reich regiment is heading our way. It is still south of here. We need to pay them a little call. Then we need to protect our villages from reprisals. This is what we are going to do."

In silent agreement they listen to his simple plan. Many of them have already lost everything; what difference will it make to also lose their lives?

*** 

"Yes. I was there. I was part of it. I watched it burn. I was a driver. I am responsible."

Georges looks at the man who knows what his fate will be in making such an admission. Heinz had heard raised voices that echoed through the destroyed house.

He admires the man's honesty. The other few prisoners taken lied. Someone else, somewhere else. Not me. Not guilty. We follow orders or we die. So they died. He had obliged them.

An empty soldier's tin on an old table occupies the space between them. A no man's land of a wedding ring, a photograph, a letter signed by 'Hannah', a child's drawing, cotton and thread, a whistle and piece of very rusty barbed wire, curved to fit in the tobacco tin. He holds the wire up to the light, examining it as though it is unique. His thumb and index finger touch as if holding a butterfly's wing.

"And this?" He pulls a small black diary from Heinz's pocket.

Heinz shrugs as does Georges.

"Fine. There is little of interest here. Hannah?"

"My wife."

"The child's drawing?"

"My daughter, Sophie."

"Age?"

"Nearly four."

"Lovely age. My daughter was nearly fourteen."

"Ah." Head bowed.

"Near the Belgian border. One of your planes."

"Ah."

"The barbed wire?"

"Retreat from Moscow. It saved my life."

"How so?" One soldier to another.

"I got caught on it. I was delayed a few minutes while everyone else walked into a trap. We had lost our tank. The Russians chased us. We were lucky. We got away. Fortunately, I was badly injured. They called us deserters for retreating. Deserters are shot for retreating. Injured men are heroes."

"The tobacco tin. First World War?"

"My father's."

Georges nods in recognition as Polish Toni enters the room.

"You need to hear this." Behind Toni they both recognised the young woman standing in the shadows.

"Come in."

"He was there," she says, pointing at Heinz with shaking hands that she cannot control.

"We know."

"But it is him." She is now very agitated.

"I know."

"No. You don't know. You have no idea. You were not there. We were hiding in the hotel. They set fire to it. We were suffocating. I dropped my little brother from the window and then my sister and I both jumped. He was standing outside at the back of the hotel."

They are all staring at the soldier who is ready to die, who would welcome death. They are ready to kill him.

"He pulled out his gun and fired it three times into the air. Then he pointed to the woods with the gun in his hand and told us to run. I expected to be shot as we ran but he just stood there; he was still pointing when I looked back at him. He did not fire. He saved our lives. He let us live."

"You are sure this is the man?"

The dark hair bobbed up and down. She is very sure. "Absolutely."

"Well, young lady. This man's life is now in your hands. May I remind you that his fellow soldiers just murdered over six hundred civilians for no reason, and one of them was your mother. You and your brother and sister are among the few survivors."

"I know, but that is because of this man."

She is very aware and knows well that Georges' family has been executed too.

"Then he is yours to deal with."

Georges leans over and places all of the soldier's belongings back into the tin. He looks at him.

106

"I think I may keep this. After all the Russians are our allies now."

The barbed wire is not modern, or of the sort the army would use. It is clearly homemade. He imagines some Russian peasant hammering the staple into place. It is a fragile piece of metal that will have no use ever again. Why would one man wish to keep such a thing? It is burnt at one end, and cut neatly at the other. Flakes of rust have formed on the table between the two adversaries. Iron returning to its native state; nothing, not even the stones last forever. Heinz looks up as the flakes of rust stop falling from the hands of the Frenchman. The shards on the table lie there like the dead men in the field on his barbed wire day. Georges reads the thoughts of a fellow soldier as he stands up to leave the room and returns the wire to the table. He places it carefully back in the tin, removes the black diary from his own pocket and arranges them next to each other. He pauses, his fingers drumming on the black notebook with the red book mark. He raises and opens the diary; two small pieces of scarlet ribbon knotted together flutter loosely onto the table. There is nothing in there except a record of what appears to be personal events and sketches that mean nothing to him. If he recognises the ribbon as the same as the one around his neck he does not show it, but he picks it up and places it in his pocket. He shows his prisoner his pencil sketches of naked trees, broken buildings, rubble-filled streets, and snow covered domes.

"Moscow?" Georges guesses out loud.

Heinz nods.

"Never been there."

"Neither have I."

The young Jewish girl looks at her hands, now containing the soldier's personal effects. She takes the very masculine-looking wedding ring and places it on her middle finger. She rolls it around, thinking of this man's family waiting for news of him back in Germany.

"I know what I want to do, but I will need Toni's assistance."

"Go, then."

They blindfold their prisoner and leave. Georges does not particularly want to kill a man who, like himself, he recognises as being already dead.

Someone in front is pulling him on a rope; someone behind trying to keep up, also on the rope. Another prisoner? Perhaps the girl? How wrong can a person be? Her voice is at the front. The heavier accent and weight behind. He estimates that they have walked for about an hour. When they stop he is aware of a brighter light. He can feel the warmth of the sun on his face and in spite of the darkness of the blindfold he knows they are in a clearing in a forest. He says a prayer for his wife and child.

"You seem decent people. Would you allow me to write a note to my wife?"

"You must be silent." The girl.

He feels the ropes grip him to a tree that is much narrower than his back. His hands are tied together. They take off his boots. He can smell the girl close to him as she pulls his head down. She places something over his already covered head and he waits for the finish. The clicking noises remind him of a rifle chamber being filled. They are going to use a lot of bullets. They are very close to him. Then the noises stop.

The light is fading and he is still alive. He can neither hear nor smell anything. The girl's light perfume has dispersed quickly in the moving air. He can hear branches still swaying in the breeze. It is now or never. He pulls on the ropes and they fall away. He reaches up and removes his blindfold. The clearing is empty save for a row of pebbles which he walks towards, and falls as his feet leave their boots, as the laces have been removed. The row of pebbles form an arrow, at the point of which is his tin resting on his diary with a page torn out. The page reads simply '*Les Allemagnes*'. The only thing that is missing is the red ribbon; his laces are around his neck with his wedding ring neatly placed at one of the tied ends; a simple tactic to delay him in the event of a problem. Laces take a long time to thread through army boots.

He takes his direction from the arrow and begins to walk towards his own lines, knowing that he has been spared by the same man who was wearing the very scarlet ribbon with the three rings he had left behind in the rubble of the church. The very man whose son that he now understood he had shot as an act of kindness. Understanding and explaining what he did is going to be very difficult, and he does the only thing that gives him solace. Before he returns to his regiment he starts to write down everything he has witnessed, including his own confession.

***

The vantage points of Mount Gargan are completely occupied. It is to be a major offensive. Georges has waited for this moment. They have thousands of men and women ready and waiting. He has given a very simple order that everyone can carry out. Do the job you have been given to do and stay put. No heroics. Do not chase them. They have to be stopped at all costs. He is content to die but he will stop them. Then whoever is left will go to General Leclerc's aid in the south of the

Normandy battlefield. Stick to the plan, destroy the supplies; kill Germans if possible, but most of all slow them down. They all know what he means by this order. They have now been joined by many of the soldiers that faced the Germans in 1940. They have an army of some 20 000 men and women. The Germans are moving forward without tank support; they have already moved north and are waiting for their supplies to catch them up. The Germans believe their intelligence that the population is subdued. But this part of the population of France is ready, ready to die for the freedom of France, ready to right a terrible wrong, ready to do everything they can to delay the German advance from getting to Normandy.

*** 

The road at the foot of the sharp bend is now impassable. A supply column of forty or more trucks is burning end to end. The Maquis cannot believe what they have done. They have routed an entire German force of nearly a thousand. This is what a massed attack can achieve. At the edge of his hearing he can hear his soldiers rounding up the last Germans caught in the forest. They ran. The mighty German Army ran from the local peasants. They left behind their trucks of munitions and petrol. They had let the supply column pass across the first bridge and as it approached the second bridge they blew both bridges, trapping them in a small area.

Polish Toni turns up with one of his female admirers in tow, a broad smile on his face, an open bottle of wine in one hand, the girl in the other.

"For Poland," he says quietly, taking a large drink and not offering it to anyone else. "For my parents and my sisters." Georges watches. He thinks Toni is becoming more and more French by the minute.

"Let it burn. Let them know what we can do. Any other Germans moving north will have to come through here and we will give them the same. First get ready to disperse to the villages. They are to be defended now." Georges stands up to survey the scene below. Single shots can now be heard. Each one indicates another dead German.

"We have killed hundreds of them, Georges. Some of the guards are SS. They were not expecting it. They ran. The SS ran. We cut them down; maybe they tried to surrender, but I don't speak German," he lied.

"But these are not the men who destroyed Oradour. I want them, too. I need to meet all the Maquis again. Round up the senior officers and find out how many people we lost today."

"They lost many."

"They lost their supplies. No gas for their tanks. That is the real victory."

***

A commander of Das Reich is thinking exactly the same thing as the first of American tanks cross the ridge, moving quickly to close off the escape route of the fast retreating German army. Georges can see them in the distance mostly hidden by the hedgerows but the long radio sticks are showing. The single line of German tanks, low on fuel but still in formation, are about to engage the Americans in a surprise attack. This is the moment Georges has been waiting for. His ambition is one squeeze of the trigger away. It will also wake up the Americans, who appear completely oblivious to the force less than a ten minutes march to their rear. Georges touches his breast pocket and notes that they are still there.

A very slender, almost skeletal face comes into focus. Its form is clear against the black uniform. As usual this man is in the lead tank, brave but foolish. Georges is ready. The last of the Maquis are ready. Everyone he knows has volunteered for this final mission, but he knows that most of them need to go back to their farms. Toni and his crew are ready. The charge on the road is laid. Two mortars and one anti-tank round ready and waiting. Then they will have the usual ninety seconds to hit hard before leaving everything and making their escape from the final action.

Georges is about to fire when a huge explosion rocks the lead tank. The tank stops at the exact spot and it loses its nearside tracks in a deafening roar, giving great pleasure to Toni, who is already moving away. The second tank is already moving to push the road block out of the way, ignoring the escaping crew who ejected the dead officer as they left. The well-trained Maquis fire their two mortars, causing the machine guns of the tanks to swing in the opposing direction. The Germans have still not fired. The Maquis scatter. The blocked road and high hedges are making the dispersal of the tanks difficult. The Americans are now frantically moving their tanks into some kind of fighting formation. It will not be long before this section of the road comes under fire.

Georges waits as the German tanks are now still making their way around the damaged vehicle. There is now no sign of the Americans. They are now waiting in their own trap in the woods. He has seen them slip away into two flanking formations on either side of the road, making ready to swoop on the column. One part of the Falaise pocket is about to be slammed shut.

He walks down towards the damaged tank. Without his rifle he looks like any other Frenchman looking for shelter, as if caught up in a place he does not want to be. The sounds of battle start as he finds his target in a ditch. He turns the dead body over with his foot. He needs to see his face. There is no doubt. He takes two photographs from his breast pocket;

absolutely no doubt. He rips one of them up and pins the other to the blood-soaked black uniform of the officer of the Das Reich regiment. He places the man's hands on the photograph and then for no reason that he can explain takes the Iron Cross from around the man's neck, puts it in his pocket and returns to his vantage point. He will burn no more villages.

Smashing his rifle, he throws the remaining bullets into a nearby stream. He stands up to leave and watches the remaining German tanks being chased across the small rise. He notes with satisfaction that most of the remaining burning hulks have black crosses on them. He tears up his papers and buries them. He removes his new papers from his bag. He is once again the very ordinary teacher that left Picardy four years ago. He has one thing left to do but his daughter will still have to wait. He looks around and checks that everyone has gone. The dead German officer is still in his ditch. He starts to walk towards the rendezvous point. He knows that another German tank column is on its way. Georges now has no past. The only photograph of his wife and son is now pinned on the medal breast of the dead man. On the back of the photograph Georges has written 'Oradour'. Georges has finished what he set out to do. The regiment known as Das Reich ceases to exist as a fighting force as the Americans now complete his task for him. The destroyers of Oradour have now been destroyed. Justice has been served in full.

His partisans have gone home back to their villages and farms, back to their previous lives. It is late but there is still a harvest. The north of France will recover quickly. In the Haute Vienne the women have been busy in the fields with their men away. The Germans have retreated back to what is left of their country. Oradour is gone too. The souls of some places are never meant to recover. This soul left the day the soldiers came.

# PART FOUR

Heinz is this close to going home but he is distracted by a noise coming from further down the track; everyone else makes for the exits at Dresden Railway Station.

He walks towards the noise, faint at first, like a murmur, coughing and wheezing. It sounds like his grandmother in her final days. It sounds like the noise that cattle make as they go on their final shuffling journey to the slaughterhouse. It sounds like death.

He sees the labels on each of the wagons: Terezin - the new re-settlement ghetto for the Jews. Everyone now knows what this means for anyone selected for deportation. He thinks briefly about allowing them to escape. He takes his notebook out from his pocket and finds a sheet at the back. He begins to write.

"Nothing but trouble there, friend." A railway guard, still doing his job, appears out of the morning mist. "On your way now before I start to be suspicious." He shines his light down the track. "The station is back there, where you belong."

He passes closer to the wagons; an appalling smell greets him. "No one will ever know," his small voice tells him.

The tick-tack of the junction points are lulling him to sleep and he smiles as his train takes him further west, away from one set of unresolved problems to another, but he does not want to be in Dresden, and being back in action stopped him thinking. As his train continues to blow away the early morning winter mist from its tracks he wonders what they will think about his notes pushed under the cattle doors of the train. He returns as the guard walked off down the line checking that all was well. Heinz quickly removes the three transit signs and exchanges them for a set meant for other wagons destined to go in the opposite direction. What will they make of an artwork delivery in Terezin and three hundred Jews in a spa town in Austria? He hopes they received his message. He hopes they will be ready when the doors are opened. He hopes they believe his simple note:

*'Change of destination. I hope you will find the salt mines good for your health. When the doors open be ready to go and move in every direction. Good luck.'*

He signs all three messages, *A friend.* He can still feel the indentations of his pressure in the page underneath. He removes it and tears it into very small pieces. He flushes it down the lavatory. This is to be his last entry into his memoires. He meant to give it to his wife for safekeeping, but changed his mind; He did not go home and now knows why. As he is rocked to sleep by the returning train taking him back to his final battle he realises how such a small event as having a pencil and paper can mean to the lives of others, and just how much fear still remains.

\*\*\*

Hannah's brother is pleased to see that his sister and her child are not there and although the names of Hannah and Sophie are called out there is no response. He has found a space for his wife and son near a door so they will have some air. The smell is already appalling. Soon it would be intolerable. Over the years as a railway man he found that good journeys went quickly and difficult ones slowly. He knows that this one will be difficult. He has managed to keep some water and a small amount of chocolate, perhaps enough for a day.

"We need to get organised." His wife nods at his quiet words. He manages to lift their small son onto his shoulders. The crowd quickly releases themselves into the small, vacated space.

"We all need to do this," he shouts to everyone in the wagon. "Lift the little ones onto the men's shoulders and let them lie across you and your neighbours. Then we can let the children sit down for a short time. Anything else you are carrying put on the floor." No-one moves.

"We have to help each other if we are to survive. Look at your children - already they can barely breathe." Still no movement, everyone is holding their little bit of space, waiting for others to make the first move.

"Listen to this." He reads out the note that he has found on the floor. "We can all survive this if we just help each other. Perhaps you can make a start." He looks at a similarly-aged man with two children. They manage to lift his little girl on to his shoulders. "Good man. Now you and you."

Suddenly there is more space. "And we will take turns at the walls. Let's help the older people there now." More complaining.

"This is my space."

"You can have mine." A young woman shames a young man into moving.

"Anyhow, who put you in charge?"

"I did. I worked on the railway. I know these trucks. We could be in here for days. We need ventilation. We must share our energies, our food and water. If anyone has a better idea, say so now. If we pull together we can make it."

"If the note is true. It could be a sick joke."

"I believe it is true."

"What choice do we have?"

"Death."

The women in the truck are already getting things moving and small spaces are appearing, allowing air particles to penetrate the spaces, enriching the atmosphere with much needed oxygen, removing excess heat, lowering the level of tension in the crowded car.

"Has anyone managed to keep a knife or something similar? We need to dig a hole through the floor."

"I have a large pair of scissors."

He held his hand out for the scissors.

"I will dig the hole." An owner keen to keep the tools of his trade. "Where do you want it?"

"Right there in that corner. The wood is usually softer there as that is where water often congregates."

"What about the other trucks?"

"We could try shouting the same message together."

"They will have to take their chances. We cannot help them."

He brings the railway map of Germany and Austria to his mind. On the image he traces the possible journeys they can make to the south and lists in his head the population centres. He remembers it like the announcer at his home station. She has perfect diction and is standing next to him.

"So," he says to his wife. "You are going to announce the names of the stations as I give you the final destination. Then we might know where we are going. It will give us time to prepare." It was a game they had often played at home while they had both been training for their roles.

The weak February light tells him that they are going south and west and hopefully to their freedom. They will need luck if they are to make it. The Americans are in the south and heading their way. Through the small ventilation grill he is able to study the familiar countryside. And he thinks of the number of times he has travelled this journey. He is on the last deportee train to leave Dresden. They quickly reach Litomerice and it seems his worst nightmares will come true but then the train, without losing speed, lurches towards another set of tracks that are not as familiar. But he knows exactly where they are going and it is not to Terezin. Pizen comes and goes and then, just as quickly as they have travelled they stop; there is an eternity of human heat and smells, lack of water, children crying, adults whimpering and sighing, silly questions to which there are no answers.

His wife moves their child to a more comfortable position.

"Where do you think we are?"

He lists the towns they have passed through while she was sleeping.

"It sounds like we are south of Prague."

She thinks for a moment and agrees that they are probably near Pizen.

They both know that they are in Czechoslovakia and probably as far away from the fighting as they can be. It is unlikely that they will have to go back into Germany. Thirty-six hours later they are across the border and into Austria.

***

He knows he will get one chance at this and it will not be pleasant. They are either in Linz or close by. He begins to lower himself through the hole in the truck. It has been used for everything, including a toilet. He thinks he could stand a little excrement if it meant freedom for his family and everyone else. His wife looks at him and nods as he loses his footing on the axel and falls to the ground. He is out but with a damaged ankle. No time, he thinks; must do this right now. He works his way around the truck to the side facing the embankment. He is experienced enough to open the door quietly before working his way further along the train. He has done this many times but not with a broken ankle. The pain is shocking but the alternative is worse. The younger men are lifting their families and others out of the three trucks. There is much hushing and child noises as they are awakened from what was for them a normal night's sleep. The pitch blackness both assists and hinders.

"Does anyone know which direction to go?"

"We walk further along the track in the direction the train is pointing. We must keep to the very edge. Leave everything that is not necessary to survival," Hannah's brother says.

The following morning they are found by a Catholic priest. They drank his holy water and spent the night on his benches but he actually knows exactly where 250 Jews can go.

At about the same time a rather confused policeman is wondering what has happened to his delivery of paintings. At first he thinks the thieves have broken in but is then quickly aware of some of the things left behind: the smell and the mess congealed on the wheels. Either way he knows he will be in trouble so he closes the cattle truck doors and seals them. He orders that they be taken to the sidings of a nearby salt mine, which is exactly the same place the priest has taken his new parishioners.

***

Hands used to physical work are moving quickly and logically. No effort is wasted. Germany laughed at the pictures of the garden-built air raid shelters that the British constructed, but Joseph can see that what they are doing is sensible. The curve of the metallic roof is a perfect deflector of exploding gases and small projectiles. The corrugated design gives it great strength and it is cheap; it requires no supporting structure. It is literally one sheet of metal formed in the shape of a letter U. This is what he thinks is the greatest strength of the British: making sensible, calculated moves. This simple structure sums them up. This is supposed to be a Germanic trait but somewhere along the way they lost it amongst the triumphalism of victory. There is no metal to spare now in Germany; everything goes to war production. There is nowhere to go, either. His logical mind calculates the best angles and placement of the doors he removed from the house; as many escape holes as possible had been included in his plan and the embankment of soil would help to deflect any blast. It would stop glass shards and small pieces of rubble, but of course anything nearer would mean death, but at least they would be outside and not buried alive in the rubble of their own home.

"They will not bomb our city, will they?" Hannah asks. Her father shrugs his shoulders.

"They will do whatever they think will win them the war in the shortest time possible. We no longer count in their calculations."

They continue to carry the door to the hole he has dug and put it in place against the wall of the trench. Sophie is putting her bucket and spade, which has never seen a beach, to good use covering the sloping door with the soil as she has been instructed to do. He has lined the trench first with slates taken from the outside toilet roof and a tarpaulin to give some further damp-proofing. A borrowed wooden fence provides the final place they will sleep on. They will have a measured sixty-centimetre space to live in and it is still beneath ground level. He has calculated that he can kneel in this space and still push upwards with his back. The smell reminds him of trench life in his war.

He is pleased with his handywork. If their house takes a direct hit there will be nothing anyone can do, but he knows that he has done everything to protect his family. He needs two more days to complete the work, but daylight is still short in February in Europe.

***

"Delightful child." He is holding Sophie in one arm. "Stop wriggling, young lady, you can go to mommy in a moment. Keep still, or I will have to hurt you." Hannah tries to hit him but she feels a familiar grip of her wrist; and he notes the missing wedding band.

"What do you want?"

"Well, apart from an evening with you, my little Jewish Princess, I want to speak with your father. We need to come to some arrangement about his future, and yours, and of course this one." He releases his grip. "Where is he?"

"My daughter, first."

"In a while." Hannah flinches as he strokes her face. "Getting a little thin, my lovely."

She walks to the back of the house and into the garden. He follows her.

Her father is busy trying to complete the garden air raid shelter. They have completed the cellar as instructed by the local order. He is a man who likes to have a fall-back position.

"You should not be doing that. The order is to build in your cellar. Anyway, they will never get here."

He looks at the man holding his granddaughter.

"Do you know who I am?"

Joseph nods. "I know who you are and I have already obeyed the order. I am an old soldier."

"Do you know what I do?"

He nods, clears his throat and spits on the frozen ground between them.

"Do you know why I am here?"

"I can guess." They both look at Hannah.

"I need a housekeeper."

"Look somewhere else."

"You do not understand, my friend. I am now in charge of rounding up the last of the Jews in our fair city. I have a great deal of influence. I can take all three of you for a trip now, or you can stay here and they can come with me. I have a safe place for them." He puts Sophie down.

"Drink?" says Hannah's father. "I have just one bottle of my own cherry schnapps left."

Fatso looks at him. "What will my friends think? Drinking with Jews. They even think the child is mine." He laughs.

Joseph goes to the cellar and collects the last of his special brew. The recipe had been his father's. He realises that it would have been his father's birthday tomorrow, St Valentines' day. His poor father had carried the same name, Valentin. He made the best schnapps he had ever tasted. He never got caught by his father, either. His father had taught him many things about chemicals and herbs; he is now an expert too.

He arrives back in the garden to an uncomfortable scene. "Hannah, Sophie needs her afternoon nap."

Hannah moves forward and away from Fatso's inappropriately placed hands, removing them from her hips as she picks up her child; only her husband has ever held her in such a familiar position like that. She picks up Sophie, grateful for her father's presence of mind. He, too, winces at the scene.

"We might need some coffee when you return. I have left the powder on the side."

"You must have some of this excellent schnapps my dear, when you bring the coffee of course."

"My daughter seldom drinks alcohol."

"Pity, I find women are so much more fun when they have had a drink. You know, old man, they relax. They enjoy things much better."

He winked at him.

"Coffee, Hannah. Our guest will need some at the rate we are drinking."

"I can give your daughter and her child a good life, and your names will disappear from my list."

"I am not Jewish and their names should not be on any list."

"Perhaps not, my friend, but your wife's grandmother was Jewish, and so are they now." He pointed at the house. "I decide who is Jewish now, and of course, who is not."

"I was a soldier in the last war. I fought for my country. Why are you not in the army?"

"Bit of a dickey ticker, old chap. Not fit for duty. We all do what we can."

Joseph knows exactly what this meant. "We do indeed."

Hannah returns with the coffee.

"This is very good, very pleasant. Sit with us, my dear. We have concluded our business here, I think." He purses his lips and sips the bitter coffee.

Her father stands up and whispers into her ear, "Do not be shocked at what I am about to say. Go with him. Do exactly what he tells you. All will be well. Trust me." He stands up.

"You must go now. Go with him. Get your coat and go before it is dark. I will look after Sophie."

***

He makes her walk towards the river, pushing her slightly in front of him. She is his now and he will have her at last. Her cocky husband will be fighting for his life in defence of Germany. The old man will do as he is told. He knows the score. If the husband does return he will use the same power to deport him. It will be all too easy to find an excuse to do so. He has already sent her brother and his family packing.

They reach the riverbank where she first walked and talked with Heinz, passing the place where they first kissed. She is pleased Heinz is not there. He would have killed him. There would have been no empty gun this time.

"We will sit here for a moment. Your father's drink is rather potent. Sit next to me. Closer."

He leans inwards as if to kiss her on the lips but she moves her head to one side. She may have to go through with this but she will at least save her kisses for the man whom she hopes still loves her. He buries his head into the nape of her neck. She can feel the wetness of his lips and tongue as he tries to lick her throat. He pushes his hands under her coat and starts to touch her breasts. His pathetic attempts disgust her but she is in no position to resist. He is pushing her skirt up. She freezes. She knows that there is now no going back as his hand reaches the top of her legs and pushes them apart. He stops. He has passed out and fallen across her lap. She tries to struggle free from his weight. She is pleased it is dark now. She is embarrassed, even more so when her father appears, carrying Sophie.

"Take Sophie home. I will deal with this."

Hannah looks at him.

"Now," he growls. "Go home, now. I will sort this out."

She understands the tone of her father's voice. He has now, without ceremony, pulled the man from her, and dumped him on the ground. He watches Hannah and Sophie disappear into the gloom. He starts to search the man's coat and finds his address and house keys, all the time keeping careful watch for witnesses. He removes all items of identity, finally pulling the small party badge from his lapel, flicking it into the river. He can just see by the light of the rising moon. He continues with the search until he is satisfied that he has removed everything of importance. He takes a small bottle of branded schnapps, pours the contents over the man's coat, and puts the near-empty bottle into the man's pocket. He rolls him towards the ice-cold, deep-running river and pushes him in with his foot. He has not been observed.

"And, I am not your friend either, old boy."

He watches him drift away in the rapid current. He sinks without trace. He throws the keys into the river and a small bottle with a black cross on it. Bad hearts do not mix well with strong alcohol and digitalis.

***

He waits for the moon to fall into shadow and in the darkness watches the river to see if his 'old friend' will surface. He pours out the rest of the special schnapps and lays the bottle on its side near the bench. He allows the contents to spread on the surface. It spreads like a dark cloud over the grey cobbles. Anyone passing this way will smell the large amount of alcohol in the air and assume some drunk has whiled away an evening here, if anyone really cares. If his body re-appears someone will put two and two together and still not make four. It is too late now for anyone in Germany to care about anything.

He realises that he, too, is making assumptions. It has become the new national habit. All of Germany is now making assumptions. They will all die; they will be defeated and the Russians will devastate, or rape, what is left of their country; there is no tomorrow; the worst is yet to come and survival would be worse than death. There is one fact that consoles him: the reign of the fat men is nearly over.

The night is clearing, a night when the bombers might come. They have been expecting it for weeks. Why will they bomb this city? Because they can, returns his little voice. He moves his little voice to something positive. How can he save his family? He hopes everyone left in Germany is thinking the same thing. You can no longer save the country. There will be no reprieve this time, no armistice. Everyone knows that. But you can save the people. If we can get through the next six months, Joseph thinks, find peace, have a good summer, grow food, we might all still survive. Hannah and Sophie matter. They are not yet completely damaged. You can destroy buildings, roads, crops and lives, but a spirit is something else. He realises that for Sophie this life is the norm. She, too, will have to adjust when all this is over.

In the clarity of the night air he knows he has done something wrong. He has deliberately taken the life of another human being. Something he has not done for nearly thirty years. He did it in cold blood and yet with the protective love he holds for his daughter, and the grandchild that his wife would have loved so much. He loves them for both of them. His little voice tells him he has actually done something good. The familiar streets guide him home.

Her father finds them at home, asleep. Sophie is held close in her mother's arms. Joseph puts his grandchild to bed.

"Where have you been?"

"He proved to be a little difficult."

"What did you do?"

"I gave him some more schnapps. I persuaded him that he needed to cool off and dry out. He can really drink, that one."

Hannah notices a twinkle in her father's eye. She sleeps. He makes a small fire in the grate and burns the papers of a very dead, fat Gestapo agent. In the morning he will warn his son to leave the city as soon as possible and take his wife and child to a safer place.

\*\*\*

Her father wakes her up.

"It is time."

He rushes them to the cellar. She can smell burning and hear noises she has never heard before.

"They are bombing the railway. We must prepare."

They can hear other families making ready. Her father has built a room within the cellar. It is strong and built for purpose. They put a none-too-pleased Sophie into a wet towel and then a wet sack. He ties her to her mother with an old belt. He wants to go to the bottom of the garden and into the open air. The alternative shelter is there. But they are instructed that they are to use their cellars. There is not enough space in the municipal air shelters. He has made both very carefully with at least two escape tunnels, one facing the side wall of the house under the stairway. Her father pushes them both through the hole. He is working frantically to get them to safety. He realises that it is a mistake to have tied them together outside.

"What is it, father?"

"Later," he says as he throws the wet blanket over them. Hannah becomes aware of the rushing sound of air and a great wave of pressure. He is waving frantically for them to move to the corner. He is not trying to get in. The last image she has of her father is of him half way through the hole. His arms are spread. She realises what he is doing - a stopper in a bottle.

"No, daddy. No. Get in here."

She tries to stand to pull him in. Sophie is too much of an obstacle. He is trying to stop the growing wind from sucking them all through the hole. She feels the pressure equalise for a moment. He is still waving frantically. Then he stops, smiles at her, looks her in the eyes and nods; he raises one arm and points a single index finger at her.

"Daddy, no."

She watches in horror as her father is sucked back into their cellar and disappears from her view as everything collapses around her. She never sees him again.

Dresden burns.

In the place he has constructed for their safety they are buried but safe, the fallen timbers acting as a shield. The upper floors of the house are gone too. The house has been sucked outwards. Other houses have caused their walls to fall inwards as they disappear in direct hits. They are buried alive.

The city above them continues to burn.

\*\*\*

At the edge of the sea a young girl views her future. She is in that quiet part of her life that all young women go through. She is changing from girl to woman. She knows she is changing. She is fortunate to have a mother she can talk to about these changes. She is reassured by this relationship. She has not yet learnt that her father is just as measured in his approach to life. She feels alive and confident. The space between her feet and the water grows less. The flowing tide is still moving towards her. She has a decision to make. Retreat or stand fast. She makes a different one and removes her sandals with the crepe soles. She is very aware that these are a special treat and are quite fashionable. Her parents have gone without to buy these shoes that she so wanted. Her socks are a different matter, but these, too, find their way to the hot sand.

Now she can have the experience of standing in the shallows of the ocean. It is warmer than she imagines. She has never been to the sea before. She is aware that none of her friends in Dresden have been there either. Most of them have never left the city. They have never even seen the countryside. This, too, is her first time away from home. Her parents are calling for to her to return. She can see them beckoning. It is a friendly gesture, not to hurry, but do not be too long. The coolness of the deeper water balances out the heat of the sun. Soon she will burn her feet as she retreats from the shore; another, new and unexpected experience. The sun has awakened her nature. She is aware that boys, some of whom she once played football with, have started to stare at her, but she does not know why. The boys are also unsure of why they are looking. Why do they no longer call for her to play out in the street? She looks at the older girls on the beach. She is envious of the young women with babies, but cannot explain why she has this strong emotion. A boat passes and its wake covers her legs to the hem of her dress and then to the tops of her thighs. She wonders if her mother will be angry. She knows she will not. A wave breaks on the nearby rocks and splashes her with water. She is wet.

She hears a child crying. 'Not yet.' She thinks. 'Please wait. This is too important.'

"Mama. Wake up." Hannah needs the dream to end. "Mama, please mama, don't sleep. Don't die."

The final command starts to awaken her. She does not wish to, but she knows she must. She turns and waves goodbye to her parents. She knows she will not see them again, even in her dreams, but they are both safe now. Her father blows her a kiss. He is holding hands with her mother. They look serene. They are in love. Her father kisses her mother on the lips. They are lovers. She is both surprised and pleased by this. They have picked up all of their belongings on the beach and are turning away. Lovers, her parents are lovers too. Her father raises his index finger, kisses it, smiles and points at her. They both know what this message means. She holds up her hand facing her father. She turns her hand to make the same gesture back to her father, and becomes aware that a small set of fingers are wrapped around her solitary index finger.

"Daddy," Hannah whispers.

"Mamma, don't die."

Hannah chooses to live.

\*\*\*

She can feel a weight on her chest and left arm. She knows she is pinned to the cellar floor. Her right arm is free. She can feel a small hand, which she squeezes hard.

"Mummy, you are hurting me."

Relief. Sophie is still alive.

"Mummy, don't die."

"Sophie can you move? Can you see me? Why can't I move?"

She can hear movement, and dust falls on her face. She is aware that air is being blown onto her eyes. Her daughter is blowing dust from her face; her clever, small daughter.

"Eyes closed, mummy."

Roles reversed; more brushing to her face; water to her lips. Hannah coughs; water to her eyes and face. A child's face appears through nearly closed eyes. A four-year-old is slowly bringing her back to life.

"Eyes closed, mummy."

A command; her father's tone of voice; more water clears her vision. A rough cloth dries her face; the sleeve of her daughter's coat.

"Sophie, I cannot move."

"It is nana's cupboard. It has fallen through the floor."

She can hear movements and has to let go of Sophie's hand. Methodical movement and the sound of her daughter's laboured breathing. Her legs are free. She lifts them, no pain. Not broken. More scraping and pressure reducing on her chest; she can now wriggle.

"Push, mummy."

There are small hands on her leg. She does as she is told. She is nearly free. They look at each other. Her daughter passes her a bottle of cold water.

"Granddad's not here."

"I know."

"Where is he?"

"I am not sure, Sophie. He has probably gone to get help."

"No one is here. Everyone has gone, but there are people asleep in our garden. They are in their night clothes mummy, but it is daytime."

"Sophie, we are going to play a game now. Then we can go to the garden. We will find something to eat. Can you uncover my arm? Move that piece of wood and those small bricks. Good."

Dust loosens, shimmers and falls through cracks. Hannah watches as her daughter begins to free her arm. She stares at her hands, tiny hands covered in scratches and bleeding, mixing with the dust.

"Now we can both go and have something to eat and drink. We can go to granddad's shelter. He showed me where the water is. He put some food in there too. He told me I was in charge. What is dry food mummy? Is it different to wet food?"

Hannah marvels at her daughter. She has already been outside and brought some water in.

"This way, mummy," she says, pointing to the light.

The sleeping people in the garden will never wake up. Her father's structure is intact. She half hopes that they will find him in there. She knows this will not be the case. He did not just go back through the hole. He had flown across the room, sucked into oblivion. Her father had always been there for her, for all of her life - when Sophie was born, when her mother had died, when the repulsive man had pursued her. When she was small and could not sleep, he would sit and read with her, not to her. They made the shelter in the garden together. He said it would be better than the cellar. She wished she had listened to him even more. He was older now but she can see why her mother had found him so attractive. It was not just his good looks but his charm. His laughter could light up a room on the darkest of days. His humour was never silly, or sarcastic, but it was always fun, a soft punch that everyone fell for every time. It caught hold and spread like wild fire through any room. Even girls of her age stopped and listened to him because he was so engaging. He never hurt anyone. She had only once ever heard him being abusive.

They had come for him to join the folkssturm to defend their city, which he would have done when he was ready. At first he had turned them down politely. But they had pursued him down the street.

"Look boys, I realise you are only trying to do what you have to do. So, please leave me alone to do what I am trying to do."

"What is that?"

"Survive."

"Coward."

"Fuck off you little prick," he whispered in his ear and slapped his face. "I was defending this country before you were even a light in your father's eye. Leave me and my family alone."

The other young man began to raise a sidearm towards him. Joseph disarmed him in one motion, the boy ended up on the floor minus his gun and also received a stinging rebuke that reminded him of his own father's discipline. Hannah's father dropped the gun down the nearest drain, much to the amusement and applause of the gathering crowd.

"Fuck off, morons, and do not come back. You debase everything that is good about our country. I am an old man. I have already done more than my fair share for this country." The crowd cheered.

"Anyway, we will all be dead soon."

The crowd dispersed rapidly. One thing had not changed. Defeatist talk is still punishable by death. His incorporation into the folkssturm to defend the city was not pursued. The folkssturm had no idea that part of his family was of Jewish descent.

That was the night most of the remaining folks in Dresden of Jewish descent were rounded up and placed on a train in cattle trucks. They were never seen again. They never arrived at their destination. Terezin found itself with a great many expensive paintings and no place to hide them. A small town in Austria with one policeman did not know what to do with the hundreds of Jews who had fought their way off their train and with the help of a Catholic Priest headed for the salt mines. No one pursued them. The local policeman wondered how he would explain where the paintings went or where the Jews had gone. No one ever asked him. It was all too late for such questions.

Her father had looked at her astonished face. She had never heard him swear before, let alone act in a violent way. "Let's go home and finish the shelter. You know Heinz is still defending us nearby. We must be ready for him when he comes."

She looks at the shelter and knows that her father will not be there. She checks the people in the gardens for signs of life, knowing it is futile. The homemade air raid shelter is just visible in the debris. Had her friends and neighbours been making their way to it?

She remembers the flowers at her wedding. As with all brides she had thrown her bouquet keeping the ones her father had made from his own garden. "Throw these," he had said. "And we will put the flowers on your mother's grave." She still had the dried flowers from her father's garden. White rose petals forever preserved in her grandfather's book of poems.

The other flowers had eventually made their way to their rightful place. Next to her favourite poem are the flowers her father had picked himself for her day.

She looks at her fingers. Her wedding band has gone to some thief for a small amount of food. She imagines the wedding band next to her mother's ring as she had worn them on the night they were married. She had never felt that way before. She had stretched out on their bed. Their bed. Their room. Her friends had warned her that the first time a man and woman are together can be painful, but this had been wonderful. She had wondered when it would happen again, when he returned to the room. She had never seen a fully grown man naked before. She took his hand and pulled him towards her. "I have to go," he said. Duty calls." She pulled him harder, into her arms and into her body. "Duty can wait for a few moments." The second time was even more wonderful than the first.

Then he was gone.

Now she is waiting for him to come home again. She knows he will if he is still alive. She looks at their daughter still sleeping. The importance of all things has changed. Life has been whittled away. You can survive in a small space if it provides shelter. You do not need stairs if there is no upper floor; nor a kitchen, if there is nothing to cook or cook with; wardrobes if you have no clothes.

"Mummy, why are you crying?" An unconditional love given by a child that cannot be beaten, or destroyed. She loves her daughter. It is enough, more than enough. She hears the air raid warnings again. "I will not let them beat me. I will survive." She cried as she sat in her father's garden. She could see him waving to her as she played as a child where her daughter now plays.

"Mummy, why are you crying?"

There is no one else. She manages to find occasional eggs and makes use of last season's vegetables from the frozen ground. The rosehips are a good source of vitamins. The drink she makes from it is Sophie's favourite. She has learnt so much from her father and still cannot believe she will learn no more from this good man. He deserved better. "Medicines are everywhere," he had told on more than one occasion. If only they had used his outside shelter.

"Daddy," she whispers.

"Mummy, where is granddad?"

***

Heinz has taken to wearing his dark glasses even on the cloudiest of days. He tells himself he is protecting his eyes even though the winter sun this far north is very weak. He is protecting his soul, or what is left of it. He lives amongst the damned and is fighting for the scraps of Germany. His wife and daughter live on one of the scraps no more than three days' walk from this point. The few active men know this, too. They, too, are near their end. They have written their last letters home, many never to be posted, most never received. Amongst those still able to fight are mostly boys wanting to be like men; to die for their country is still the most honourable thing they can think about. Dying for your country is very easy to arrange.

In the darkness of dead sleep his worst nightmares prevail. They are flying over in their thousands, dropping their bombs without thought; no one resists. In what is left of free Germany cities burn and more people die. He sees the death of his mad friend, Adi. His lovely, mad friend killed by a simple solitary shell fired by their own soldiers, exploding the walls of the church in which they sheltered. A roof beam falls and crushes the face of his lovely friend. He searches his pockets for personal effects, knowing that there is now no one to send them to. There is just one clean, white handkerchief.

In his disturbed sleep he imagines what his friend will say to him.

Heinz passes him a white sheet of cotton.

"How are things?"

"Not good." He coughs into the handkerchief. "But you do not need me to tell you that. We are no longer in control of the situation. We can still fight but it just means more death and destruction for nothing."

"When did we last receive a direct order?"

"Three days ago."

"Nothing since."

"The men think they have all bailed out in Berlin."

"What do you think?"

"I think they are right. We are on our own."

"I need to make a decision."

"Yes, you do."

Every effective leader needs an honest broker. They have no purpose except to be your conscience. They have no motive but have the courage to tell you how it is for the right reasons. They have no words but are your sounding board. They pass comment like a barber, mostly it is of no consequence, but sometimes they ask you the most pertinent of questions. The man in Berlin does not have this facility. His barber is too scared, as are the rest of them. Being scared of a leader is not positive; great leaders always command respect, not fear.

"Are you sure?" is the most asked of questions in any fighting army when someone needs to make a decision that involves life or death. The response is the difference between life and death.

"What do you think that order should be?"

"You will know at the time. You are very special to the men."

"As are you."

"Perhaps, but you are their natural leader."

"As are you."

"To a degree, but I do not make the decisions. I see to their needs; I hear their moans. I do not give orders. You do."

"I need to give that order now."

"Yes, you do."

"I think I will tell them to go home, that they have served their country well, but it is over. It is time to go home."

"I think they will agree."

"How can I tell them?"

"Just tell them. They are thinking the same way already. They just want to go home."

"When?"

"Now."

"They hate us you know." His friend had told him when they had finally left for Normandy. Their delay by the Maquis had been costly in terms of time lost as the invasion by the allies had taken hold.

"Who does?"

"The whole world. All of them, even our allies. They all hate us. The French. The British and now the Russians too, not to mention the Dutch, the Belgians. The Spanish and the Italians hate us too. And now the Americans. We are on our own in this, now. We cannot take on the whole world. We have bombed and destroyed most of Europe and now the tide has turned against us. And just wait until they find out what we have done to the Jews."

"The Jews?"

"You don't take on the Jews. They most of all have a grievance to remember. They never forgive anything and they have a memory as long as time itself."

"What have we done to the Jews?" He has heard rumours. He knows people have been relocated to the East, but he has barely spent three months at home in his war.

"Murdered them."

He turns to look at him. "How do you know this? What is your evidence?"

"Next time you go on leave ask yourself why are all their shops empty. Where have they gone? Why are their parts of the city unoccupied? The synagogues have all been burnt to the ground. The men in their funny hats and beards have all gone. When did you last see one? You need to take note my friend. Watch and you will see. Ask your wife. She will tell you what the rail trucks are full of and it is not food, or guns. Why are there no Jewish men serving with us?"

***

"It is time, *Capitaine*."

A young soldier shakes him awake, using the nickname given to him by his old friend Adi, in the French campaign, whose wise counsel he could do with right now.

"We need orders. The senior officers seem to have all left. There is only you."

Heinz sees the glow in the Eastern Sky in the long distance, but this is winter and it is too early for the dawn. The young soldier looks at him.

"Dresden. They have bombed Dresden again."

Four hours ago he was awake and what is left of his dream for Hannah and Sophie was still possible.

"Why?"

"Sir?"

"Do we know why all the officers have left?"

He shrugs his shoulders slightly as he turns away. His only response is muted by fear. He cannot see the young soldier's face. It is hidden behind a mask of dirt and sorrow, but his voice is young and it is clear from his tone that he is scared. Everyone is scared.

"Wait. Do you know how bad the city is?" A question to which he does not want an answer.

"No sir. Bombed all night; burnt all night."

"How old are you, boy?"

"Seventeen."

"Where are you from, son?"

"Dresden."

He nods. "Me too." It is one of the few places left where recruits can still be obtained.

"Does anyone know where the officers have gone?"

"Some of the others say they have left to organise a final defence near the Czech border."

"'Pass the word; tell everyone to pack their kit, personal possessions and as much food and water as they can. Everything they can carry. Any engineers left?" It is time to go home.

"Just me, sir."

"Bring any others that you trust to me. I need explosives experts who can destroy what we have left. Now pass the word. Assemble the men."

"Sir." A voice pleased to be doing something.

"Good luck, son."

"Thank you sir. Same to you." The young soldier raises his arm and touches his metal-clad forehead in salute. The days of 'Heil Hitler' appear to be nearing their end.

***

"It is time to stop thinking of our beloved country," he tells what is left of the company of men. "It is time to think of ourselves and families. You have served your country well but now we need to go and defend what is left of our homes and families. If you can go home go there. I have orders for all of you. You know where the American lines are. Do not die now without reason. That time has passed. The time for staying alive has arrived. My final orders are the same for each of you. Save what is left. Save your sisters and mothers if you can. All will be well. I gave you orders and you obeyed them with honour. It has been an equal honour to serve with you. You fought with courage and honour; now it is time to go home."

Heinz removes the top sheet of paper, revealing the same orders for each man beneath, and looks at the words he had written about his friend:

131

*So, why does the world always lose its most precious diamonds?*

*Replaced by strokes of the pencil that*

*Allows those who can to rub out what they do*

*And escape the damage they do to you, or you.*

*They are the bringers of joy, but like a place without a name*

*Are torn away from our gaze*

*And are removed from the love of their friends*

*That they send, they send. They send;*

*The spark of life they bring*

*In the darkness of what they leave,*

*And we are left with nothing;*

*And nothing can relight the Universe,*

*As light of itself does not bend,*

*Not even for you,*

*My friend, my friend, my friend.*

*My lovely friend.*


He closes his eyes and hopes he will always remember him as he awakens each day and what he wrote about his lovely, mad friend; but it is already too late to forget, because it has already been recorded for ever.

***

Hannah knows they have little time left. Her father is dead. Her husband is probably dead. He will not save her this time. Her beautiful city of books, of love, and poetry is gone. She still has no idea of the complete devastation of the place she has called home since she was a little girl. All of her life has been spent on these streets, except for one trip to the seaside. She picks up Sophie and decides it is time to leave the shelter. She knows they will still come for them in spite of the chaos. She knows they will enjoy it even more. They still believe that in spite of their imminent defeat they will be remembered well by the people of the earth. This, they believe, is to be their ultimate victory.

In the street the dead are piled high, like logs waiting for winter fires, piled high by the scum. She watches them moving the bodies, searching them, removing valuables and papers. In a side street she sees the body of a young woman and a small girl sealed together in a final embrace of protection and love. The scum begin to walk towards her when the air raid warning sounds again. They disappear faster than rats down a drain. How do they do that better than anyone else? The ID checks will continue. She sees a thick black coat near the woman and child. It is better than her coat. She exchanges them and covers the mother and child with her coat. In the pockets she finds the Identity Papers of the mother and child. They are frayed and torn. She is about to put them into the coat covering the bodies, when another possibility occurs to her.

***

The streets of Dresden have been cleared of much of the dead and rubble. Hannah has arrived at the bench where her father last protected her. She knows her father is dead. Sophie keeps asking for her granddad. Hannah half-expects him to meet them at the riverside; and there is a familiar figure waiting there on the bench.

"So you both made it," she says without looking directly at them.

"My father is dead." A quiet whisper for Sophie; a finger to the lips and a nod of understanding from the older woman.

"Your husband?"

"I do not know. He may still be alive fighting the Americans."

"Is your husband a nice man, a good man?"

"I suppose so. I have not seen him very much since he was in Russia. He was sent to France because of his injuries. But his letters have stopped coming."

"My husband is not a very nice man. He has disappeared but he is not listed amongst the dead. His friends have not seen him since before the bombing. They even came to my house to see where he had gone. I think they believed he had disappeared. He had many papers in the house, mainly deportation orders. He is always very careful, knew how to take care of himself, an eye for the main chance. I never really knew what he was doing at first, but one day I followed him to your house. When I asked him who you were he said your child was his and we would take her in when you were deported. He had a plan to go to some relatives in Austria and start again. I knew only then what he was doing."

"Sophie is my husband's child. I will tell you now. I have never known any other man and that includes your husband. He came to threaten my family with deportation if I did not cooperate with him, but that was the last time I saw him. That night the bombers came. He never returned."

The lady at the other end of the bench nods. "I have something for you and your daughter."

"Thank you but you have already been very kind. We would not have survived without your help with food and gifts."

"I only gave you what he stole from others, what was left over. And it was not much."

"It helped. It meant I could feed Sophie."

"I have to admit that was why I did it. It was selfish of me."

"I do not care about your motives. I have a healthy child thanks to you, even if it is for the wrong reasons."

"Look, I will share this little bit of food I have left. There is just enough here for the three of us, and then I am going away. I still have rail tickets for Austria. I hope his cousin will take me in. He always had a hope that I would choose him for marriage. I wish I had done so. I made the wrong choice."

They eat their final shared meal in silence. The increasing wind fans the embers of the dying city; fires are starting again, but there is nothing much left to burn so they remain insignificant compared to what had happened for the last three nights.

"Is your house still standing?" A common question being asked all over Germany.

"No." An equally common response.

"My house is damaged but you could still live in it if you wish. I will have no need for it and there is some tinned food left in the cellar if you get there before the scavengers do." She stands up to leave, placing a large key into Hannah's hand, picking up only her handbag, leaving the other, larger shopping bag under the bench. "The address is in the bag with the other papers I found. Good bye," she says and walks towards the smoking city.

Hannah takes her eyes off Sophie, who is playing too near the water's edge, but the woman has already passed out of sight.

"Goodbye, Helena," Hannah whispers.

Sophie looks at her. "Let's see if granddad has come back yet."

"Good idea, my angel." Hannah feels the presence of the key in her hand.

"I am in charge of bags," Sophie says. "And this is a heavy one."

Hannah pulls the bag out between her legs and opens it. There is some flour, eggs and bottles of what looks like homemade wine. A number of papers have slipped down the bag in a side pocket. She studies them carefully. They have not been signed. She looks at the mismatched names between their own papers and those on the deportation forms. She rips the names off all of the deportation papers and puts them inside her blouse. She searches frantically for her brother's name; his wife, their child. She can find no evidence; they have gone. There are two rail passes to Austria signed by the local mayor, and this is still a small part of a functioning Germany. The rest of the papers are thrown into a nearby kiosk that once sold tea, coffee and ice cream to people taking a stroll by the river. Its smouldering structure consumes the papers with rapid ease and she wishes she had done the same thing with the contents of her blouse; a final part in this jig-sawn world.

***

They go back to their hole in the ground, stopped once by a young drunken fanatic who just wants to take the bottles from her at first. When he tries to grab her for more than food or drink she swings the bag and hits him right between his legs. A kilo of flour is enough to cause any man problems, especially one who is filled with alcohol and desire. Hannah has survived too much already to allow a spotty boy to endanger her and Sophie. She deliberately smashes one of the bottles at his feet; its contents fizz and fume around the shards of glass as she picks up the neck of the bottle with a sharp pointed end and aims it at his vocal chords, causing a slight scratch on his neck.

"Come anywhere near me, and I will kill you. Do you understand?"

He nods slightly in total surrender. She is shaking as she walks towards their ruins. He is last seen holding his groin and vomiting the contents of his stomach over what is left of the iron railings of a destroyed house. She did not know she had such courage within her soul, but she realises that this is more about survival than courage.

Sophie is very pleased with herself. She had helped her mummy to get rid of the horrible boy because she had aimed a few effective kicks too. Then she had found a small black-hinged box in the bottom of the bag as she spooned out the egg goo for their meal. She enjoys the crunchy scrambled eggs and strange flat bread cooked over an open fire started with the paper contents of her mother's blouse, the final cause of concern now just another part of the city of ashes.

Sophie enjoys her mother's smile when she opens the box and finds a little note. "These are mine. I have no one else to give them to. Please keep them for your daughter for her future, or use them if you need to. Sorry." It is not signed but it is obvious that the small pieces of jewellery are personal and not taken by her husband. They are not worth a fortune but gold is always worth its weight in any difficult situation.

***

It rained bombs again during the night, and they are still at it, the scum, removing good clothes, gold teeth, spectacles, shoes, annoyed that they might be checking the same bodies. They take anything that can be bought or sold, or exchanged for food and drink. They are still checking names and addresses; still marking names off lists. They find the bodies of a mother and child, badly burnt. The mother is sheltering the little girl as best she can, but to no avail. They take the papers from her pockets and a letter. The papers are in good order.

"I thought we had got rid of all the Jews." Small man, toothbrush moustache, slicked back hair. "Except for that train load; bit of a shock that. They escaped, you know, into the salt mines they say; still looking for them. Austrians not too pleased," he tells no one in particular.

"Papers." The man with a swastika armband searches the list for their names. He crosses them off. "Put them on that pile." The logs grow higher. They still bother about Jew and Gentile even now. Yet they will all be burned together in one mass funeral pyre. Hannah and Sophie have finally been crossed off the list. Their next of kin will be informed that they are both dead. The man frowns as he sees the name and rank of the husband.

"No accounting for taste. He's not going to be pleased when he receives his little note."

***

Heinz watches the countryside passing by. It appears very much the same. There are no troops, tanks or bombs. No aeroplanes either to attack his train. Some of the men he addressed are travelling with him. There was some trouble over tickets but the soldiers simply ignored the officious ticket collector and asked if he wished to stay alive. He is surprised to notice that the train is virtually empty. He will soon realise why as he notes the large numbers of people already walking south in the fields nearby. They are leaving the burning city as he is entering it.

He looks at his black notebook in his matching hands with their filthy nails. Are they the same hands that she had so loved? How can Hannah possibly want such a stained person anyway? The mental and physical scars on him are not going to be erased, ever. He has been involved in nine months of bitter fighting with the Allies and there is to be no miracle. The sooner this is over the better. He puts the still unopened telegram in his tin.

***

136

What is left of the German Army has retreated too far and is now cut off. The Russians are laying siege to Berlin. It is a matter of days now. They are supposed to be defending this part of what is left of Germany, but he knows that this will end up as just another mass of murdered soldiers and civilians. He has informed his immediate superior officer by land line that he needed to go into Dresden to find out if his wife and child are still alive. He has been refused. He had refused to open the telegram until now. If it remains unopened it then it cannot have happened yet.

This is his tipping point for a decision he should have made weeks ago. Who knows now who will still be alive? He is now a deserter and they are still being shot. He will need a good reason if he is challenged and remembers that he still has his orders to attend hospital to have his wounds checked.

A soldier in uniform can still largely travel anywhere. He is still armed. Nothing is going to stop him now. Rumour is rife. Soldiers are deserting in their droves. As the train passes groups of people they have not even bothered to remove their uniforms; they look like they are assisting citizens, but not in the usual fashion. They are retreating with civilians as cover. It is over, but not yet finished. As he leaves the station he passes the deserted check points and notices the absence of the watching Gestapo Agents. You could spot an agent from a distance as they were the only ones who had spare body weight. The power of these men is disappearing rapidly. Later Heinz will find out that some have been shot by soldiers as they retreat to try to find safety. They, too, have had enough of these people who are the very enforcers of the fighting, but do none themselves. Try telling a real soldier that he is a coward for not fighting on when he knows that it is his actions that protect these small men who have worked their passage throughout the war by persecuting people who have done little or nothing, who have kept themselves in power by fear.

The intellects of real soldiers are now far beyond fear, past caring, as are those of many of the agents who now have extra holes in their bodies donated by the same first soldiers to get angry with them. Once it starts others follow. The people of Dresden, like so many other places, note that they may now have a chance to survive. They have to take the opportunity. They, too, can now ignore the fearsome agents, and if they need to will remove them from their way without hesitation. Retribution is a fearsome weapon in any aftermath. Dresden may be on fire but these flames are consuming evil too. They whisper messages to each other.

"Our own soldiers are shooting the Gestapo."

***

He realises that this will probably be the final time that he will return to his city. It looks as though winter had stayed late in the undamaged outer areas of Dresden; everything is covered in a frost-like white. As he walks in from the outer railway station towards the centre he realises it is simply ash. He makes his way along the familiar streets and as he progresses so does the damage. He stops to gaze at the people living in shelters constructed from the debris of their homes. They ignore his torn tunic when they would have once acknowledged it with pride. This is a people beaten beyond humiliation. In the partly-cleared streets children are playing games he does not recognise. The normal games of childhood are gone to be replaced by games of war and death. The flattened city reveals itself before his eyes. He has only ever seen such destruction once before. They were promised something that would last a thousand years, but he can only count a thousand days.

He reaches the corner where he used to kiss her goodnight. His worst fears are soon answered. On the train he had opened the telegram to receive the expected notification saying that his wife and child are dead. He still holds some hope that there has been a mistake. The facade of her parents' home still stands, an empty shell of a once prosperous home. His nearby street is gone. There is nothing left. He can see the partial remains of the church where they were married. He removes his tin from a torn pocket and takes out a shoe-laced gold wedding ring pendant. He tries to return it to its rightful place, but its looseness on his fingers matches his tattered uniform, so once again he places it back on his string and over his head, his old bootlaces holding it in place.

A small child, holding a rag doll, appears in the ruins. Sophie looks up to see a figure standing on the rubble of the house. She sees a face she thinks she recognises, but does not know who he actually is. She holds the doll's hand up and waves it at him. He holds his breath and the oil-stained envelope in his pocket. He waves back.

***

"This is your daughter," a female voice says. "Say hello to your father, Sophie."

He recognises someone who looks like his wife, but this is not the woman he married. She looks old enough to be his mother. She stands perfectly still, their child between them.

"They told me you were dead - both of you." A telegram is waved in his proffered, oil-stained hand.

"We are dead." That will take some explaining, she thinks. "Why have you come back?"

"I said I would."

"Why?"

"I had to know."

"Know what?"

"That you had survived."

"Hannah, this is your daddy. Say hello to him."

"She already has. What is your dolly's name?"

"She has no name."

"She is very pretty. Like you. Like your mama."

"My nana made her for me."

His wife shook her head.

"My father?" Again she shook her head.

"Your father?"

"No," she screams. "There is no one left. My brother, his wife and son, your family, everyone has gone. They are all dead. The city is dead. We are all that is left. Why are you here? Why have you returned? I did not expect to see you again."

"I came back for you, but we need to go now. The railway to the south is still open. There is nothing to stay here for."

"I hate them for what they did. They are all murderers."

"No. Not all of them."

"But look at what they have done. Look at it - our parents, our homes, our future. They have destroyed it. They are responsible for all of this."

"No," he says, slowly. "We are."

He thinks of a beautiful medieval village in France on a sunny afternoon in June just before they came. He remembers three scared Jewish children who ran to safety in the direction in which he pointed. He thinks of a Frenchman who lost everything and everybody, who had spared him his life, spared him for this moment in time. He reaches out to his wife, picks up his daughter, kisses them both.

As they walk towards the railway station he casts aside his torn soldier's greatcoat and hat to the ground. He takes an overcoat that covers a dead man and collects a civilian hat. Heinz opens his shabby brown suitcase and takes out his small black book and a battered, battle-worn tin. She watches his face change as he removes other small items of importance - some of her letters neatly tied up with string, her grandfather's silver pocket watch and a fountain pen, which she gave to her husband as her gift on their wedding day, and a book that he knows he must now finish reading. Sophie is already opening his partly filled shepherd's bag. He smiles at her and then, in exactly the same way as he did when he had first met her, he smiles at Hannah. He looks at her with the same expression that first touched her soul. A familiar expression from a man she now recognises again. He places his forehead to her brow. She notices the wedding ring she gave him as her token of love, not on his finger but around his neck, suspended by old boot laces. He, too, has noticed the absence of rings on her hand.

"Is there anything you need to tell me?" He draws breath, his opaque mind finally clearing of obsession and hate.

"No. I have always loved you. We have been waiting for you. I traded the rings to feed our child." She can always read his thoughts.

From around his neck he takes his yellow wedding ring, first placed there in the forest by a young Jewish girl who had also given him back his life, and lowers the frayed loop of the bootlace holding the gold ring around Hannah's head. Heinz realises that his wedding ring is so thick that they will be able to forge two new rings at some future date.

"I love you," he says.

"I know," she replies.

"What does 'I love you' mean?" a small child asks.

"It is like this," he says, as he picks her up and squeezes them all together.

"Good," says the small, firm voice.

She smiles at her daughter's response and the sensation of the pressure of his arms as they are both released from the power of his embrace, and allows them to start to move away from what is left of the still-smoking city to become part of humanity again. He finds her hand in his. He squeezes it and she smiles. He returns her smile and so finally she has the answer to her question.

He also finally thinks that he realises he may have an answer to his question of what the author of the unread book meant by 'It was the best of times and it was the worst of times.'

\*\*\*

He fights for a place for them in the corner of an overcrowded compartment. He has used his soldier's uniform for one last time to make use of their inherited rail ticket passes. Now it is their turn to be shipped like cattle, but this is not an open wagon. It is very cold but they are alive and have some shelter and a little food, which they share with others who then return their generosity. The children quickly settle to sleep on parental knees as the shared food and human heat of the compartment take effect; children sense the feeling of security from their parents which has surrounded them for the first time in months. They slip into a deep sleep. She is astonished at how quickly the devastation gives way to undamaged farms and fields like the Germany she remembers from her childhood. As they pass through the darkness and despair he thinks about telling her how he has reached this point but does not. He gives her his diary and tells her that everything she needs to know is in the book. He has left nothing out. She looks quickly at the pages and the neat writing of a man who has never really left her or the child they made between them.

"I will read it later."

She smiles as she needs to sleep. Her head is carefully cradled on the shoulder of her husband. Sophie is using their laps as her bed; her father's bag is her pillow. The diary is put safely with other important items that will map out their future. Hannah even realises that she can one day claim their true identity back. He kisses his wife on her head and she sees him smile as a sleeping Sophie takes hold of his hand.

"I have not seen you smile like that for a long time."

"No, you have not," he thinks as he realises why the author chose the order of the opening lines of the book so carefully, and as other survivors from the conflagration, tell them to hush, he voices one final opinion.

"This," he whispers to Hannah and a sleeping Sophie, "is where it finally begins. This is the best of times."

The following day they pass the church where her brother, his wife and their son found shelter under the benches of the old church. They, too, will soon be reunited with each other.

# PART FIVE

## The Punishment of Adolf Hitler

As people all over the world begin to think about celebration and believe they have survived to see their loved ones again, one man is loading a gun which has seldom been fired. He is shaking with anger and disbelief and can only just put the bullets into the magazine.

"You have betrayed me - all of you, all of Germany." The empty words fall only on the ears of his dead wife. "You are all responsible for destroying our beloved country. You are all cowards." He raises the gun, bites down on the capsule, and fires.

As his conscious mind recedes into the darkness that eventually takes us all, he can see very bright pinpricks of light; they are the faces of people of all ages, sizes, races and sexes, and he is especially aware of those near the front who had been recently persecuted. They are all wearing a large yellow star. They are all pointing upwards. He thinks at first that they are raising their arms in their millions in salutation to him, as they have so many times before, but they are not. They are pointing away from the light, their extended arms moving in slow arcs, similar to the trajectory of a small ball thrown by a child, a fired shell, or an arrow launched to obtain maximum range. Had they come to greet him, to reassure him? A small child steps out from the crowd and signals to him to come forward. He can see that she has a number tattooed on her arm. She shows him to a large concrete room with a huge metal door and gives him her yellow star. As he enters, the crowd applauds. It is now the biggest number of people he has ever seen together. They are still arriving. The crowd stretches in every direction as far as the eye could see. For a moment he hesitates but the child is insistent.

He likes children. He did not have a very happy childhood himself. He enters the room and the light disappears as the door closes. He does not like the dark. It is his fear of the trenches and being buried alive that causes this fear. But he is not alone as there are many others with him, many of whom he does not know, but there are many that he does know and they know him. They no longer wish to be seen with him, but that is not an option.

Outside everyone knows him and on the pure white walls the children of the world are busy writing in all the languages of the world:

Auswitz

Belsen

Coventry

Dresden

England

France

Germany

Holland

Italy

Jew

Katyn

Leningrad

Munich

Nurembourg

Oradour, the little girl with the number on her arm writes.

Poland

Quisling

Revenge

Stalingrad

Terezin

U boats

V rockets

Warsaw Ghetto

Xawery Czernicki

Yugoslavia

Zyklon B

Inside the room he thinks at first that he is alone and the only sound he can hear is a hissing noise just above his head which sounds like a gas escaping from a broken pipe. It is a noise that he will hear for the rest of eternity. But his punishment is not yet complete. It has not yet even begun. His uniform starts to scratch him as he sweats continually. There will be no relief from the itching darkness or the smell of the gas that temporarily blinded him in the Great War. He had called it the swimming pool gas.

\*\*\*

A small boy waits patiently outside to take his turn. He does not yet know what he will write on his space on the wall. He has been told that he will know when the time comes. He picks out his yellow crayon as that is his favourite colour.

'Small boy from Holland and his lovely mummy,' he writes and signs it, *Pieter.* The queue moves on but there are millions more in the line. Young boys and girls with very blond hair write, *you took our lives too.* They write in German for that is what they are. One of the older boys writes, 'I loved my father but he murdered me and my brothers and sisters, and our mother. Who gave him the right to poison us?'

Their father is stood on the left of the man with the small moustache. Their wives are to the front. On his right is a man who desperately wants to clean his spectacles but he cannot move his hands. He will have to wait for his very round glasses to demist, but it is cold in here. It is the perfect temperature to preserve the dead. Every person who died at this man's hands will form their own separate queue to ask him why he murdered them. His view of the world will remain opaque until they have finished their personal questions - and they died in their millions in his concentration camps. Only then will his hands be released to clean his spectacles.

\*\*\*

From the inside of the concrete bunker Pieter thinks he can hear crying. His mother said to write something nice. Another boy, much younger, is standing next to him. He is wondering where his father and sister are. He is pleased they are not here. He, too, is assured because his mummy and nana are with him. He does not yet know how to write and so he has no crayons to write with. He whispers this to Pieter, who shows him his crayons and he picks out a red crayon. Red is his mother's favourite colour. She always wears a red ribbon in her dark hair. Their mothers wave to them and Pieter starts to write for his new friend.

'Oradour is a small village in France. One day some very bad people came and when they left everyone was dead.' Pieter writes his friend's name, his friend's mother's name and his nana's. Then, after further whispering between the two boys, added a final word: *Why?*

Inside the bunker they still wait in their rows - row upon row upon row. Nothing appears to change or move. If it does it is infinitesimal. There is no sound except the hissing noise. One person is also wondering why he is on the wrong side of the wall. He is answered immediately but only he hears the response.

"You put all the Jewish children from France in a cattle train without their parents. Some of them were still in their nappies and you dare ask why you are here? Many of them cried for their mummies and still you did not answer them. They were alone in the dark. They were babies. They died in their thousands on those trucks and at Auswitz without comfort or anyone to care for them. And you dare to even ask." He recognises the voice as his own.

"If it were not me it would have been someone else. They would have killed my children."

"You have failed your test. You have tried to excuse yourself. You have forfeited your place in the line. Go to the back."

"Why me?"

"Because the children of the world have a right to justice."

"Just who do you think you are?"

"You."

The man who ran the trains from Paris to the concentration camps finally sees the train he sent with the children arrive at their destination. As the doors open the children have already gone, but the smell is appalling. He thinks he can hear the children's voices singing happily but he is wrong. Their cries and the smell will be his for the rest of time.

Everyone else in the bunker asked a similar sort of question once, but had never repeated it. They know precisely why they are here waiting. They do not want to go to the back of the queue again. So they keep their thoughts to themselves and hope that their torment will soon be over.

"I was only following orders," says another.

"You burnt my village to the ground and so until it is rebuilt you will share the unhappiest of my memories."

He looks at his blood-covered hands and thinks he can feel blood running down his shirt; he thinks he can hear the sound of children playing on a midsummer's day that will last forever. He recognises this sound as in the background he can hear a church bell tolling, as it did on the day it fell and rang for the last time. The sound grows louder and louder very slowly, forcefully penetrating the very soul of the man who destroyed the village. He keeps wiping the blood of the children onto his shirt, trying to clean his stained hands, but it will be there forever. I, the village, warned you I would have my revenge. So, just for you, let us start with all the children you killed. You can share their images forever. Enjoy their names and the lives you took from them. Let us start with the unborn child who would have been called Marie.

He closes his eyes and the children start to line up again. History rewinds. He will not close his eyes again for the rest of eternity. No matter how tired his eyes grow he knows that if he shuts them for a moment it will all start again. This is the thousand years that the little man who remains at the back promised them. Only here it is not thousands, not millions and not even billions or billions of years.

When everyone has finished writing their messages the people on the inside will have to read them all. Only then will a final solution be found for what they did to others who are not part of this. He knows he will be the last one to read the words. He has all of eternity to wait and say he is sorry. In the darkness the little man in the brown shirt with swastika emblem, who still has his moustache, moves from one foot to the other, going from side to side but never forward, and he waits, and he waits, and he waits.

\*\*\*

Someone else is waiting too. She waits at the gate every day and still the road is empty. The delivery man comes with supplies the sisters cannot provide for themselves. His brother had been the local priest but he had been killed in the evacuation trying to help the soldiers on the beaches and in the sand dunes. This man was allowed out of Dunkirk - the area still occupied by the Germans - to make his deliveries to the convent.

"The war is over you know," he tells the figure at the gate. She nods. She always nods. He thought she was simple and as he hands her the bags of flour and sugar he again wonders if she is simple.

"No salt today, Lucy. Do you have tomorrow's list?"

She hands him the carefully written note. He is astonished to find a request for a radio.

"A radio? That may be difficult. The Germans are still patrolling the area. They do not seem to know that it is all over. They have stopped fighting everywhere except here. Typical that we are always last on the list for anything. Are you sure Mother wants a radio? Is she taking up dancing? That would be funny to see.' He stops, realising that he is now out of line. A radio; anyone would think the pope was about to speak.

Much later, the delivery man returns with a passenger. She is still standing at the gates when she sees him climb down from the back of the wagon. Something prickles across her skin and locates itself at the back of her memory. She can feel the weight of a man's great coat over her, warming, protecting but now slipping away. She remembers a smell and sounds of screaming - a woman's voice, her mother. Her face appears and disappears and she cannot find it again. The fog lifts, and then it is clear and complete. The first time she has seen her mother's face for years. Again it returns clear and complete and smiling. She is speaking to her but there are no words. She thinks she is saying we love you always. She is saying goodbye, why?

From across the road the face of the passenger is closing in on her and she closes the gate. A blurred face appears out of a soldier's coat; it begins to take on a form but it appears to shimmer in her eyes like the road surface on a hot day. A young man's face is smiling at her, a reassuring face, pleasant. She reaches out through the gate and touches the new face as the astonished delivery man stands to one side. The all-encompassing weight of the black coat that she has worn since her arrival at this place seems somehow lighter. They both catch her arms as she starts to fall.

Once again Frank finds himself carrying the same person. He had known she would look different and had not expected to recognise her. She is older and heavier but here she is. A serious-looking young nun appears at the evident scene of distress.

"You cannot come in here."

"That is what I was told the last time I was here."

The nun looks carefully at Lucy and then at Frank. "You have been here before, soldier?"

"Yes; I need to see the Reverend Mother. She will know who I am." And as nuns often do, the very lady appears at the gates.

"Bring her to the infirmary. And how are you, young man? It has been quite some time. I wondered if you would come back."

"I told you I would return."

"I know, but you said she was your sister."

"Lost in translation, Mother. Will she be alright?"

"I think it will be difficult for her. She has barely spoken to any of us until recently. She has few memories. She remembers you for sure. She has stood at that gate every morning for years. The sisters call her the 'keeper of the gate'. It is a -"

"Biblical reference. Yes I know. I would like to see her now if that is possible."

\*\*\*

She is aware of the warmth of another human being's presence. Another hand holding her hand very gently, a hand that is attached to a sleeping man in a chair next to her infirmary bed. She lifts his hand. He really is asleep. The hand has the dead weight of a child deep in slumber. She studies his face in the early morning sun streaming through the high windows. His breathing is steady and disturbs the flow of dust particles floating in the silence of the room.

For the first time she is awake and the rest of the world is asleep. An inner peace settles on her and she studies his face more carefully. She notes his loss of youthfulness and the small scars which litter his face. She wonders how this had happened. She decides it is a nice face. She slips her hand back into his hand, his presence now making the whole room feel safe. She notes the elderly nun at her station sleeping soundly, undisturbed by the emotions of others in her care.

\*\*\*

A little later, in another part of the convent a conversation takes place, one that has occurred more than once before, usually between the nuns.

"What are we to do with Lucy?"

"Reverend Mother, I do not know."

"She has no name, no papers. She can stay here for now but our Lucy is no nun, she needs to be in the world where she belongs. She looked for you, of course, perhaps unaware of what she was looking for, and now here you are. Why are you here?"

"I feel responsible for the fact that I brought her here."

"I know, but do you feel anything else?"

"Such as?"

"Love perhaps."

A frown.

"Of a man for a woman?"

Another frown.

"When I first saw her she was very young. It does not seem right. She is a lovely young woman but I am much older."

"She is about eighteen and you must be twenty-five or twenty-six. *C'est bon*. She will still be lovely when you are very old like me."

"I will do anything I can to help her. It must be possible to find some family."

"Not if they are not searching for her. They believed her to be dead."

"This is solving nothing."

"No, but I have an idea." He follows her down the corridor and into the library.

"I have done this many times before for babies, you know." She remembers the risks taken for the Jewish families as she opens the registry. Baptism records falsified. What will she say to her maker when He holds her to account? Well, He had been Jewish too.

"Now she has a name and an identity. If she agrees, you could marry her. She will then take your name and you can take her with you into the world where she belongs."

*** 

"Lucy, I need to explain something to you."

She sees her soldier - her saviour. She feels she has waited for this man forever, but he does not seem to see her as his love. She is unaware of any feelings he may have. She is there for his asking but she needs proof.

"Is this just for convenience?" Lucy looks at the Reverend Mother for an answer.

Two old hands reach out from black folds. They are palms up.

"For you both to decide. Does it matter?"

"Why did you come back?" she asks Frank.

"I had to know."

'What did you need to know?"

"That you were alive. That you did not die."

He describes to them of his love for his sister but does not give her name. He tells of her death and how he could not bear it to happen again. Saving her is like saving his sister. This time he can do something about the outcome. He can make a difference. For his sister it was not possible. He explains to her how her smile had re-assured him as she covered herself with her father's black coat.

"I have no knowledge of a life except this one."

"I understand."

Who is this man? In her heart she knows she has waited for him all these years and he is breaking her heart. She has dreamt about him every day of her life. Tears move from her eyes of their own accord. He reaches for her and holds her close. This is what she wants but her hands are caught against his chest. She cannot show him so she tells him instead.

"You saved me. You came back for me. You are my only contact with the past. I need your help to find my family if they are still alive. With you I can find out who I am."

"Your family were alive when I last saw them. But I think they believed you to be dead. They had to go quickly. They left you to save your brother."

"I have a brother?" She shakes her head in astonishment but there is a heave of the shoulders too.

"They left together, but went in a different direction. I called to them to try to explain that you may still be alive but they did not understand. We could not stay as the planes were returning for a second strike."

"Where did my family go?"

"That I do not know." Then he whispers in her ear, "I came back for you because I feared I had lost another soul and it was you who saved me. You gave me a reason to live, to go on. If that is not love then I cannot explain it."

"Is it the love you have for a sister, a mother?"

"What I feel for you is not the same as my sister. It is more than that. It is quite different. You are who I am."

In front of a smiling, aged nun he brushes the curls from her face and kisses her gently on the lips. She returns his kiss with a smile.

The white hands appear from the folds again and begin to write on the paper with an ancient pen. A master forger she will be in her next life.

\*\*\*

The sisters take an altar server's alb and turn it into a peasant's wedding dress. They braid her hair with red ribbon and white gypsy. A posy of red and white roses, taken from her own garden, complement the simple dress and her natural beauty.

Frank has already acknowledged the enormity of what he is about to do, but when he sees her he knows it is the right thing. Her shyness catches his soul and if he were not in love already he is now.

"You are so lovely," he says.

"So are you."

Lucy notes the slight frown and makes a note to ask him later if there is still a problem. He knows what his father will think about his marrying a Catholic girl, in a Catholic church by a Catholic priest. His father is a bitter man for reasons he does not yet understand and can only guess at. But there is no question now to answer except those of the same wedding vows that people have made from time immemorial.

She places her posy of flowers at the foot of the altar as she turns to leave with her husband and the reassuring smiles of her sisters.

\*\*\*

The rains fall on Oradour. A small seed germinates in one of the walls. As it absorbs moisture it expands and with the additional warmth of the air, it germinates, so now it must force its roots to find space, forming fissures in the rocks. The rocks accommodate this by allowing small grains of sand to fall from the wall to start their journey again to the sea. May blossom sweeps to the ground, rolling like open parachutes in the gentle wind that follows the rain. The echoes of the war have ceased for this village. I can hear no more the sounds of battle. The keepers of the death villages have been found and have taken their place along with the others. Beneath the walls the doors close and leave just a little space for those who think they have got away with it, but they will arrive here eventually, as everyone with evil in their souls will arrive here sooner or later. My visitors come to show their respects and they are unaware of what I, the village, have done, as they are unaware that they share all of their memories, good or bad, with me. I have not reserved a space for him. Some return to say they are sorry. In spite of fighting in an evil war he has been allowed to keep his soul and will live out his years with Hannah and Sophie and their new child, who has just been formed in his mother's womb. I will not call him to account for what he did that day. Others may pass judgement on him for that. I hope he is treated well. Not all of my villagers died that day. They were not all born of me but they found shelter in my walls and were happy here. They escaped the nightmare, and unlike the others, were given another chance.

After all, unlike another place, my walls have stood for a thousand years.

\*\*\*

Polish Toni has a final mission. He needs to trace a young Englishman who saved his life, who carried him for fifty kilometres. He knows his other saviour died. He had watched him float away, face down after the attack, but he had seen Frank being pulled into a small boat. Now the moment has arrived. In his pocket are the tattered remains of the notes Frank made about him on the journey to Dunkirk.

"Remember me?" He says to the sandy-haired man who appears at the door. Toni holds up his left hand with its missing finger - a wedding band would have to be worn on his middle finger. Frank had dressed that wound often enough.

"How did you find me?"

"It was easy enough." He hands Frank the papers in his own writing. He had recorded the wounds, injuries and treatment for any future doctor and he had signed them in his clear handwriting.

"Your legs?"

"I still have them thanks to you and your mate."

"Who is it?" A foreign female voice comes from within the darkness of the house.

"A friend from the war."

"He must come in." Toni is briefly aware that he recognises the accent.

"My wife is French," Frank says as he introduces them. "Lucy, this is Toni. We travelled together to Dunkirk. Toni, this is Lucy. In fact, he was there when you and I first met. He was the man on the stretcher. He was unconscious at the time."

"So was I - unconscious that is."

Toni is staring at her, shaking his head. "Do we know each other? Do you know me?"

"You cannot possibly remember each other. But Lucy is aware of your story."

Again he shakes his head. "No, but I need to hear all about it. My memories are very vague until we arrived at the beach. I have no memory of what happened after the attack."

"Which particular attack? The one at the beach?"

"No, the one where you met each other, the one where I was unconscious. I remember stopping and hearing the sounds of chaos but little else. The next thing I was really aware of was the nurses in the hospital at a convent. Proper nurses, you know." Frank smiles at the jibe.

"I was in a convent too." She holds her husband's arm. "You are not the only one he saved that day - and the ones to come, too." She places her hands on the very noticeable bump.

"Our first."

"He is rather embarrassed as I was only fourteen when we first met, if you could call it that. Our real first meeting was when he came back for me. I am nearly twenty now."

"Where is the convent?"

"The outskirts of Dunkirk. It was not liberated until the end of the war. The German garrison held out until after the surrender; strange thing that - Dunkirk twice over."

"Lucy is an unusual name for a French girl." Toni, for some reason, begins to sound agitated.

"Lucky Lucy," she says and smiles at her husband again.

"I guess I gave her that name. She has no memory of the events that took place there or before. When I returned to the crossroads she was still there covered by her father's black coat. She remembers seeing me and then I had to take you to the nearby convent; and while you were being treated I went back. There was no one else there. It was deserted. I nearly missed her. It was dusk and the light was failing. As I was about to leave I saw the coat. She was beneath it. She was alive. She was still warm to the touch."

"He carried me on his back to the convent in the village, all that way again, and after he had carried you." She looks at both of them. "The next day he left with you, but without me. He did not even say goodbye. I guess there was no time, but I knew he would come back for me again. He told me so, or maybe it was the sisters who said he would, but I knew that he would one day see me again. I cannot remember anything else. I have no memory of my childhood, my parents, and my family."

She walks across the room to a small dresser and opens the drawer. She takes out some Rosary beads and a medal.

"This is all I have; this was around my neck when Frank found me and these were in a pocket of the black coat. But they hold no memories for me."

"I think we need to go to France."

"I think I need to go to hospital."

Three days later Lucy delivers their son, Jacques; going back to France will be delayed for a while.

***

"I know you. I have seen you before. Right here in this village." Georges speaks to a figure rising from placing three red roses on the steps of the destroyed *Hôtel Avril*.

"I had hoped you would not recognise me. The others, they may know who I am too." He nods at the four figures walking down the slight slope past the ruined post office and hotel; one of the women is carrying a very small baby in her arms. He knows of all of them except the baby.

Georges turns and looks up the road at the figures: Polish Toni and his wife Elizabeth and another couple. He does not know the other man but his breath catches near his heart, which misses a beat. The other lady is the very image of his dead wife. She walks towards him, almost hesitating, but then a direct look that the same lady used to reproach him with. She starts to lift her son towards him and he picks up the small bundle from her arms.

"His name is Jacques." A distant memory of a lost brother returns, perhaps it had never left.

She notices the hands of the man who is now holding her son. He, too, is now gazing at a remarkable similarity - long elegant fingers, yet strong and powerful - as she takes her son's hands out from under his covers. He nods.

She looks at him again.

"They say you are my father?"

"Am I?"

"Are you? I cannot remember. I have no memory of many things."

He looks down at his dusty, worn boots, and tries not to raise his head, but he allows his eyes to move upwards. He sees a tall, slim, elegant young woman. The lips he recognises. Her beauty has come from his wife. He meets her eyes and he knows.

"Do you remember what you were called when you were a little girl?"

"Someone used to call me Loulou. I think it was because of the first sound I made when I was a baby. Did you give me that name?"

He stares at his own eyes in another's body. They suit her. The silver of a mirror is not needed. He knows he is staring at his own partial reflection. He is looking at his own child.

"It is your name from the stars."

He reaches out to her, a single hand opened flat, palm upwards. She falls into his embrace, the very small baby boy squashed happily between them, and looking over her shoulder at the German he has forgotten about; Georges nods to him.

"Why are you here?"

"I came to say I was sorry." His wife takes his hand and that of their daughter.

"We should leave," Hannah says.

"Daddy, why are all these buildings broken?" the young German girl asks.

"I will explain later."

Toni looks at Sophie, and in his excellent German explains, "Your daddy saved this lady's life right here." Jacqueline, the oldest of the surviving children, joins the growing throng.

"I assumed the three of you had died. I saw you fall in the distance."

"We were carrying our little brother when we all slipped and fell down the bank."

As Sophie begins to play on the steps, her father turns to Frank. "I remember you, too. I saw you at the crossroads. I thought you were stealing from the bodies. I was about to shoot you. Then I saw the Red Cross on your armband." He turns again to look at her; she is still in her father's arms.

"And the last time I saw you this man was carrying you on his back. You were a young girl. He was on his own. I think he must have returned for you."

"I know."

She stares at him and can only nod as memories burst like a torrent. This is her village, her home, her father. She remembers putting crab apples into the post office box to annoy the postman. She turns and looks at her father. She looks behind her at the burnt-out tower of the church, at what is left of M. Denis' fine wine shop, the *Hôtel Avril* in a ruined state, the boy's school where she had waited for her little brother.

"What is my name?"

"Julia. Your name is Julia."

She nods and takes from her pocket a medal - the Croix de Guerre - and some Rosary Beads.

"I think these are yours," she says. "As am I."

"As am I," a little voice thinks.


The land has nearly healed itself. Cooled air particles roll across uneven surfaces, shifting and moving in the uneven landscape, the scars disappearing into the tree line, rocks shimmered in the heat, expanding, contracting releasing the surface, the same rocks being worn away by frost and snow as they froze and expanded in the heat that always follows the cold. Only time is changed here. Buildings are falling inwards and outwards, slowly returning to where they came from. A church, still recognisable in the devastation, holds no aura of love or compassion. It is grey on a day when a strong light would normally mean definition. The buildings appear to not want to be there. No presence. Prayers trapped that afternoon. Not answered. A silent melted bell does not call worshippers to prayers. It, too, has no answer. That will come later. From a distance everything looks normal.

His daughter stands where he had once stood when he returned from his war, surveying her village, eyes squinting in the strong, clear light, looking at the tram road where 200 SS troops walked down one summer's day. She tries to remember her village on such a summer's day before the soldiers came. Her memories have only just begun. Julia is in love for the first and only time in her life. She feels the pride that her father has for living and life. She lives close by and I, the village, am now ready to pass on my soul to her safekeeping. Unlike me she is not tired, but vital and ready for the future. She is taking stones every day. Soon I will be gone. Where am I going? She brings me her child and I can feel again the child's hands brushing my surfaces. The hands are cool and careful. They are large hands for such a young child. The child takes some stones and places them in his toy cart. In a garden, in a new village, I am there, and the same gentle hands have surrounded me with plants. One of my stones has a new inscription:

*Souviens-toi*

*Recueillez vous*

*Remember us*

I recognise the child's breath on my stones, and finally I sleep.

# A WORLD AT WAR

Down this road on a summer day in 1944, the soldiers came. Nobody lives here now. They stayed only a few hours. When they had gone, the community, which had lived for a thousand years, was dead. This was Oradour-sur-Glane in France. The day the soldiers came, the people were gathered together. The men were taken to garages and barns, the women and children were led down this road, and they were driven into this church. Here, they heard the firing as their men were shot. Then they were killed too. A few weeks later, many of those who had done the killing were themselves dead, in battle. They never rebuilt Oradour. Its ruins are a memorial. Its martyrdom stands for thousands upon thousands of other martyrdoms in Poland, in Russia, in Burma, China, in a world at war.

Introductory lines from the highly acclaimed ITV Series *World at War*.